Why was his shy nephew taking such an unusual liking to this mysterious stranger? Luke rubbed the sudden tension in his neck.

"Hey there, Cody." Alexandra patted his back, and when he stiffened, she tucked her hand under her thigh. "I bet you're hungry."

Luke caught her eye and watched her beautiful, broad smile fade into... Was her expression contempt...or lust? His blood suddenly ran a little hotter. If things continued like this, he was in trouble. Big trouble. His old dating tendencies—to play the field and be serious about no one—were too close to the surface, and Alexandra was making it a challenge to keep his promise to his sister. His promise to be a better man. Cody came first. He would not go back to juggling a different woman each weekend.

He joined them at the counter and took the empty seat on the other side of his nephew. "How's your morning been?" he asked Alexandra.

"Great. And I haven't caused a bit of trouble...yet."

There was no way he could miss the mischievous grin she attempted to hide.

Dear Reader,

Welcome back to Oak Hollow! I'll admit, I'm always happy to revisit my fictional Texas Hill Country town. *In the Key of Family* is the second book in my Home to Oak Hollow series. This story was inspired by a few of my family members as well as some of the students I taught when I was an early childhood teacher.

Oak Hollow police officer Luke Walker is adjusting to his role change from fun uncle to full-time guardian of his five-year-old nephew with autism. Luke has forgotten he's renting out a room, and the person who shows up on his doorstep is far from the young man he'd expected. Alex Roth is a strikingly beautiful woman with a guitar, art supplies and a free spirit that doesn't fit with the stable home he's vowed to create for his nephew.

Alexandra hopes to discover something about her ancestry, and she's giving herself one last excursion before taming her wanderlust and settling down to use her music therapy degree. The last thing she expects is a handsome but very opinionated officer who challenges her and a little boy who believes she's Mary Poppins. Can a young boy help them make music together?

I hope you enjoy *In the Key of Family* and will visit Oak Hollow for the third book in the series when it releases in the fall of 2021.

Happy reading!

Makenna Lee

In the Key of Family

MAKENNA LEE

HARLEQUIN

SPECIAL
EDITION

HARLEQUIN®
SPECIAL
EDITION™

PLEASE RECYCLE · THIS PRODUCT IS RECYCLABLE ·

Recycling programs
for this product may
not exist in your area.

ISBN-13: 978-1-335-40493-0

In the Key of Family

Copyright © 2021 by Margaret Culver

This edition published by arrangement with Harlequin Books S.A.

For questions and comments about the quality of this book,
please contact us at CustomerService@Harlequin.com.

Harlequin Enterprises ULC
22 Adelaide St. West, 40th Floor
Toronto, Ontario M5H 4E3, Canada
www.Harlequin.com

Printed in U.S.A.

Makenna Lee is an award-winning romance author living in the Texas Hill Country with her real-life hero and their two children. Her writing journey began when she mentioned all her story ideas and her husband asked why she wasn't writing them down. The next day she bought a laptop, started her first book and knew she'd found her passion. Makenna is often drinking coffee while writing, reading or plotting a new story. Her wish is to write books that touch your heart, making you feel, think and dream.

Books by Makenna Lee

Harlequin Special Edition

Home to Oak Hollow

The Sheriff's Star
In the Key of Family

Visit the Author Profile page
at Harlequin.com for more titles.

To my amazing son Benjamin.
You make me proud every day!
And your caring nature with your brother
influenced this book's hero.

Chapter One

Alexandra Roth stumbled back when the Acorn Café door fired open, and a tall cowboy rushed out with a large bag of ice over one shoulder and a twelve-pack of beer under the other. He sidestepped just in time to avoid sending her sprawling onto the hot sidewalk, and his obsidian eyes sprang wide.

"Pardon me, ma'am. So sorry."

"It's...okay." She barely managed to squeak the words out past her surprise and a flare of attraction.

Were all the Oak Hollow residents this polite? And this smoking hot? She adjusted the guitar case over one shoulder, pulled out her cell phone and snapped a photo of him walking away. The historic town square created the perfect backdrop to frame his powerful form. Tight maroon T-shirt over bulging muscles, worn jeans, hat, boots and enough swagger to get a girl's motor revving. A genuine cowboy in the flesh. Not something she often saw back home in Manhattan.

He paused, and she thought she'd been caught taking his picture, but after a few beats he continued across the street to a black truck. Attempting to look nonchalant, she leaned her large rolling suitcase against a post and sat on top. Her movie-star sunglasses were the perfect concealment for stealthy observation. The cowboy handled his purchases like they weighed nothing, but his flexing muscles told a different story as he put them on the tailgate and leaned in to drag over a cooler. Ice cascaded and chimed like musical notes over the glass bottles.

Alex didn't want to take her eyes off him long enough to dig out her sketch pad, so she'd have to use her memory and the one photo to paint his image. A hot breeze fluttered her billowy sleeves, and she wished for some of his ice to cool her heated skin. Beer wasn't her drink of choice, but putting a cold amber bottle to her lips sounded pretty good about now. Maybe she'd run into him again, and they could share a drink, or a meal, or…

The star of her developing fantasy slammed his tailgate. His eyes were hidden in the shade of his cowboy hat, but the wide grin he shot her way was as clear as Waterford Crystal, and she knew she'd been caught staring. Rather than looking away in embarrassment, she returned his smile. He gripped the brim of his hat in a sort of cowboy salute, then climbed into the cab and started the engine. It wasn't the first time she'd been caught observing someone whose likeness she wished to capture with paint.

Once he'd driven down Main Street, Alex studied the covert photo on her phone, only feeling a smidge guilty about taking it without permission. But you couldn't see his face, which was unfortunate because it had been a really nice face—all angles and strong lines, tan skin and a bit of dark, sexy stubble. It would be the first watercolor painting she'd work on once she got settled. If she didn't melt in this oppressive Texas summer heat. She gathered her long mass of auburn hair, twisted it into a messy bun and secured it with two paintbrushes from the front pocket of her guitar case.

If her few minutes in town were an accurate depiction, it was no wonder her mother had spun romantic tales about her summer in Oak Hollow. The place she'd met the love of her life. The place Alex had been conceived twenty-five years ago. She pulled out the envelope of her mom's photos and held them up for comparison to the real thing. The oak trees were bigger now, but the location was unmistakable. In the photo, her mother, Kate, stood in a white gazebo with her arms around a handsome, blond-haired young man, both of them smiling at one another like they'd hung the moon and lit the stars. She'd caught her mother looking at her that way over the years, but there was an underlying sadness hidden in her smile.

After tucking the pictures safely away, she typed the address of the room she'd rented for the month into her phone and set it to walking directions. Alexandra continued her trek from the Oak Hollow bus stop with her guitar bouncing rhythmically against one hip and the wheels of her rolling bag clacking along the sidewalk behind her. The town square, with its historic buildings and white stone courthouse, gave way to homes ranging from Victorian and Craftsman to midcentury modern. Children rode bikes down the quiet streets and the air smelled of freshly mown grass.

Was it possible any of her unknown relatives lived in one of these houses? Maybe aunts, uncles or cousins? Possibly her grandparents? Although, her mom hadn't painted a very kind picture of her dad's parents, who had not accepted her. She'd been an out-of-towner and hadn't been deemed appropriate for their son. Someone they feared would lure him away to the far-off big city. Even so, her mom had never forgotten about or stopped yearning for the man she loved.

Alex hoped her time here would be long enough to make a few discoveries about her ancestry, and the father who died before he knew his summer love was pregnant with their child. But she'd have to be careful about her inquiries and respect her mom's wishes not to give away her identity. Being a twenty-five-year-old secret baby was no fun.

The GPS led her down a shady street that curved around a huge oak tree, which must have started growing a hundred years before the road was constructed. At home in Manhattan, only a few small trees grew in the teeny, tiny outdoor space below their balcony. To see nature this grand required a trip to Central Park. Alex inhaled the spicy sweetness of a cluster of roses hanging over a white picket fence and released a long, cleansing breath. Fingers crossed, this trip would be the last hurrah she needed before taming her wanderlust and settling down to use her music-therapy degree.

Her phone rang, and she stopped to answer. "Hey, Mom."

"Hi, honey. I just wanted to make sure you made it there safely."

"I did, but I think I've gone back in time and landed in Mayberry." Her mother's laugh held a note of unmistakable sadness that tugged on Alex's heart.

"Sounds like the place hasn't changed."

"It's just like you described. Are you sure you won't join me here?"

"I'm far too—" Loud, high-pitched grinding drowned out her mother's voice.

Alex pulled the phone away from her ear and waited for the noise to die down. "What's going on? Aren't you at work?"

"Yes. I'm in my office between patient appointments. That sound is proof that I'm far too busy to leave the medical practice. We're having some of the plumbing repaired."

"Sounds like the perfect time for you to get out of town. It could be the closure you never got."

"I'm fine. Don't spend your vacation worrying about your mother."

"I know you'd tell your patients to do exactly what I'm saying. Heal so you can love again. You should take your own advice once in a while."

"Alex, I'm not broken, and I don't need a man to be happy with my life."

Her mother's standard answer sounded like a rote response that held no real meaning. "Fine. But I can't promise I'll give up trying."

"Tell me about what you've done so far."

Alex adjusted her bags and continued walking. "The bus ride through the Hill Country was beautiful. The wide-open landscape is dotted with sunflowers, and the crests of the hills gives way to domed blue heavens. Not a skyscraper in sight to obstruct the sweep of nature. I did some sketches on the ride."

"I knew you'd see it with your artistic eye."

"Right now, I'm walking to the house on Cherry Tree Lane where I'll be staying."

"Please, be careful. Remember everything you learned in self-defense class and always be aware of your surroundings. And if anyone asks about why you're there—"

"Mom, I remember everything we talked about." She took a breath and made a concerted effort to keep exasperation from her voice. "I won't embarrass you."

"I'm not worried about that. I just don't want

you to be disappointed or get hurt by anything. Or anyone."

"My father's family might not even live here anymore."

"I'm sure they do. The Hargrove family was a long-standing and integral part of Oak Hollow."

"Then I shouldn't have any trouble gathering information without bringing attention to myself."

"Honey, I'm sorry I've put you in this position. It's not fair, but I don't know how else to handle a delicate situation."

"I get it. I'll be fine."

"Have fun. I love you."

"Love you, too. Talk soon." Alex hung up, excitement and nerves jangling in her belly.

She might not be able to join in at a Hargrove family dinner, but she could at least learn something about them and get a feel for the town where her father grew up. And put the polished rock she'd brought on his gravestone.

Luke Walker seriously considered kicking his own ass for driving away from the intriguing woman outside the Acorn Café. He'd almost gone back to talk to her after icing down the beer, but he'd promised himself he'd be responsible and focus solely on his new parental role. He glanced in the rearview, guilty that he hadn't at least offered her a ride. The suitcase made it obvious she was a visitor, and as one of Oak Hollow's peace officers, he should've been more welcoming, but controlling his natural tendency to flirt was proving difficult.

Women, especially redheads like the beauty he'd almost flattened against the sidewalk, had a history of causing him heartache. And she'd looked to be exactly the type that had gotten him into trouble of one sort or another. Stranger or not, the old Luke Walker would've stopped and invited her to the party, but that guy only had himself to consider.

His life was different now. It had to be. A child's future depended on him.

Luke jerked to a stop at a red light, and the full cooler slid across the bed of the truck.

Damn it. I need to pay attention.

He did not need residents seeing one of their off-duty cops running a red light. This was exactly the way his troubles with the opposite sex often began. Something little like an embarrassing traffic slip or forgetting which woman he had a date with on a given night. A distraction of the female variety was the last thing he needed right now.

Making the switch from Uncle Luke to full-time guardian to his five-year-old nephew, Cody, had to be his primary focus. He'd been proud of his role as the fun uncle, but the unexpected position of dad had been thrust upon him, and he was struggling to live up to his own high expectations. Learning to parent a child diagnosed with autism was something he took very seriously.

His sorrow was deep for the older sister who'd become a mother to him after their parents died.

The least he could do was to raise the son Libby had loved with her whole heart. Cody was easy to love, but Luke was terrified he would fail at the role entrusted to him. He often woke in the middle of the night, panicked that he'd make a wrong decision. His nephew needed extra attention and a whole lot of understanding and patience.

Luke glanced skyward at the billowy white clouds. "I promise to do my best, sis."

Someone honked and he realized he was sitting at the green light, doing exactly what he'd feared and embarrassing himself. He pulled forward and continued toward home, and the birthday party his friends had insisted on throwing for his twenty-eighth. They said things like "Have some fun like you used to, Walker. Cody needs you to be happy. You have to keep living…"

But every time he tried to have fun, he'd remember the day he received the devastating phone call that Libby had terminal cancer. Then the day she died. And the day they buried her next to their parents. His heart thundered in a chest that felt three sizes too small. He gripped the Swiss Army knife on the console hard enough to make him curse, but that was better than the panic attack that threatened.

I'm the one in charge. I can't fall apart.

He pulled into his driveway and parked around back, near the detached garage. He'd used his last excuse to go out for beer and ice, and he couldn't continue to sit in his truck while his house was filled with friends here to celebrate. But damn he dreaded going back inside. A house full of people reminded him too much of the gathering after Libby's funeral. Hardest morning of his life. Make that second-hardest. Having to watch Cody say goodbye on the day she died was definitely top of the list.

"How can I be everything he needs?" His only answer was the ticking of his truck engine as it cooled. "I need to get my ass in there. Being a man means doing a whole lot of crap you don't want to do."

He slammed his door, hoping the exertion would blow off some of his frustration, then heaved the ice chest from the bed of the truck and pushed his way through the back door. After putting it beside the kitchen table, he went to find Cody.

His boss's new wife, Tess Curry, pointed behind the sofa. "He's in his safe spot. I couldn't get him to eat anything."

"Damn. I shouldn't have left."

"You needed a minute." Tess squeezed his shoulder. "Anson and Hannah will be here in a few minutes, and my sweet girl will no doubt get him to come out or crawl in there with him." She glanced at her watch. "I need to get something out of the oven."

Luke adored Anson's wife and five-year-old adopted daughter, Hannah. They'd become the family he needed. His boss—and friend—was an example of the kind of parent he wanted to be. Anson had taken to raising a child with Down syndrome like he'd been born to it. Every time he had the errant thought that Tess and Anson would make better parents for his nephew, guilt and shame sliced deep. He desperately wanted to be a good father. He could and would do this thing right. And he was lucky to have people he could ask for help.

Luke kneeled at the end of the sofa and peered into the space behind the furniture where his nephew went to escape the chaos of the world. Cody sat cross-legged, staring out the front windows as he rocked himself back and forth.

Luke's shoulders wouldn't fit in the narrow space, but he stuck his head in. "Hey, buddy. Are you hungry?"

The small boy glanced in his direction but didn't meet his eyes. "Hot dog."

"Want to help me get it and see what else looks good? There's lots of food on the table."

Cody shook his head.

"Okay. I'll be back with your hot dog in a minute. And your friend Hannah will be here soon."

Cody didn't respond. Instead, he drummed his fingers on the windowsill, and stared out as if he was watching for someone.

Luke feared he was waiting for his mother to come up the walk. And it broke his heart.

Chapter Two

Thankful for the shade of arching tree branches, Alexandra stopped on the sidewalk in front of the blue-and-tan Craftsman house on Cherry Tree Lane. Cars, trucks and a few motorcycles crowded the driveway and curb. Had she rented a room in a party house? She liked to have fun as much as the next girl, but too much of a good thing could turn sour. She brushed a lock of hair from her eyes and rolled her suitcase up the brick pathway to the front door.

Half-barren flower beds flanked the curving front walk and called out for her to tend them and mix in a bit of color. Maybe even some medicinal and edible herbs. Even though this yard wasn't hers, and she was only here temporarily, maybe the landlord would appreciate the gesture and allow her to play in the dirt. A yard like this was something she didn't have at the apartment she shared with her mother. And the chance to have more to work with than a few pots was exciting, especially since she stayed off their third-story balcony, which triggered her fear of heights.

She lugged her suitcase up three steps and onto a covered front porch that would be the perfect place to relax with a cup of morning coffee. Twin rocking chairs sat on one side and a white porch swing hung from the other. The sweet face of a small, dark-haired boy peered out a front window, but then disappeared from view. A second later, he opened the door and stared through the mesh of an old-fashioned screen door, like she'd only seen in movies.

"Hello there."

He pushed the screen enough to make it swing halfway open and then without a word, he quickly ducked back behind the couch.

She stepped over the threshold into… What was this? It sure wasn't a wild keg party. The living and dining rooms were filled with people, ranging from young to old. She tucked her suitcase and guitar into the corner beside an entryway table and took in the scene. A birthday cake that read *Happy Twenty-eighth* and several gifts covered the dining-room table. Laughter drifted among the mingling guests and the savory scents of food made her stomach growl.

"Help yourself to food in the kitchen." An older woman moved past as if Alex's appearance was an everyday occurrence.

Rhythmic thumping came from behind the sofa and she glanced down. The young boy sat hunched in the space, tapping out a rhythm on the windowsill. Her empathy gauge kicked on, and she sensed the pain and sorrow within the child. Alex kneeled and wedged herself into the small space to sit beside him. Was this little boy in trouble and sitting in time-out, or was it something more?

"What's your name?"

He did not glance her way but stopped rocking and tapping.

"I'm Alex, and I'm new in town."

"Alex," he whispered. "Alex, Alex, Alex."

"That's right." She heard movement over her shoulder and glanced up.

"Cody, here's your..." The cowboy from the town square crouched down so that he was nose-to-nose beside her. "It's you!"

"And it's you." Her pulse fluttered before taking off at a gallop. Surprise shifted his handsome features, and the friendly grin he'd flashed earlier disappeared. His full lips pulled into a hard line, but that didn't stop her desire to stroke the hint of dark stubble along his strong jawline, just to see if she could ease the tension. If she painted this version of him, the artwork would be brooding...and sexy.

"Who are you? And what are you doing here?" he asked.

The deep timbre of his voice pulled her back into reality, and he did not seem to share her desirous thoughts. "I'm Alex Roth."

The little boy reached around her for the plate of food in the man's hand.

She passed it between them then continued, "I'm looking for Luke Walker. I've rented a room in this house, but I seem to have come at a bad time."

"You're a girl."

She chuckled, enjoying the quick change in his demeanor. "Wow, you're really observant. You should be a detective."

"I'm a police officer."

She laughed, but he didn't. And there it was again. A slightly menacing expression. "Oh, you're serious. My landlord is a cop, too. Guess you work together?"

He stood and rubbed a hand across his eyes. "Sorry. I just assumed Alex was a guy."

"My real name is Alexandra."

"To be honest, I forgot about renting a room. That was before…" He glanced at the little boy. "You okay, Cody?"

He nodded and bit into his hot dog, then used his free hand to continue tapping out a tune on the windowsill.

"So you're the Luke I'm looking for?"

"Yep."

"Wait…" Everything he'd said clicked in her brain, and her stomach dropped. "What do you mean, you forgot about renting a room to me?"

"We should take this conversation to a different location."

She glanced back at the little boy and joined in on his tapping. "I'm glad I got to meet you."

Cody flicked a glance her way then changed the rhythm. When she followed along, he grinned.

She crawled out of the tight space and let Luke pull her to her feet. The spicy musk of his aftershave tickled her nose and a lovely tingle warmed her hand. She didn't want to let go, but he jerked his hand away and shoved it into his pocket, sparking another flicker of disappointment. "So the room is no longer available?"

He motioned for her to follow him away from the child. "My nephew lives with me now, and this is a two-bedroom house. I'm so sorry I didn't contact you. It just went out of my mind after my sister, Libby, died."

"Oh, my God. I'm so sorry. She was his mother?"

He swallowed hard and cleared his throat. "Yes."

That was the cause of the sorrow she'd sensed in the child, and the tension on Luke's face revealed his own struggle. But this turn of events left her hanging out in the cold, or in this case, the Texas summer heat. "Is there a hotel in town?"

"There's one, but it's booked solid because of the annual Fourth of July celebration next weekend. It's the seventy-fifth anniversary of the picnic, and some of the special guests have arrived early for reunions and stuff."

"Oh. Well…" *What the hell am I supposed to do*

now? She'd planned to be free-spirited on this trip and take things as they came, but this was going a little too far. She had no intention of sleeping in the park. "I came here on the bus, and if I'm not mistaken, the nearest town is at least a half hour away. Without a car—"

"I'm not going to kick you out onto the street." He stepped closer and lowered his voice. "I promise I'll make sure you have a safe bed to sleep in tonight."

Is he offering to share his bed?

Warmth flared in her core. Sleeping with a stranger—even if he was as tempting as a lemon-drop martini—wasn't her thing. Although…she *had* promised herself new experiences. She shook her head and pulled herself from dangerous thoughts. She couldn't get a good read on this cowboy, and his attitude toward her seemed to be bouncing between attraction and avoidance. "Whose birthday are you celebrating?"

"Mine." He shrugged. "I didn't want a party, but I guess everyone thought it would take my mind off the hard stuff."

"It's not working?"

"Not really."

She propped her hands on her hips and glanced around the room. "Want me to send everyone home?" His tentative smile grew into a full grin that made her body tingle in all the right places.

"You think they're going to leave at the request of a complete stranger?"

She stepped closer to his heat, happy to see the lines of tension ease around his mouth and eyes. "You never know until you try."

"Come have something to eat and we can sort this out."

She followed him into the kitchen and eagerly chose a glass bottle of Coca-Cola from a bucket of ice. It was cold, sweet and the best thing she'd tasted in ages.

"Walker," an older man called out to him. "I need you to come see this."

"Help yourself to food," he said. "I'll be back in a minute."

The yellow enamel top of the kitchen table could barely be seen through numerous glass dishes of home cooking. The buffet was irresistible and within moments her plate was heaped with a variety of Southern delights. Dessert would require a second trip.

"Hi, I'm Tess Curry," said a woman with long, chestnut hair and a huge smile. "Welcome to town."

"Thank you."

"I remember what it's like to be the new girl, but everyone is very welcoming. Let's find a place to sit, and I'll give you a brief rundown of Oak Hollow and its residents."

Tess could be the perfect person to ask about the Hargrove family, but she'd have to be careful and not seem too eager for specific information. Alex added a scoop of potato salad to her plate and followed the other woman to sit on folding chairs in front of the fireplace. "Let's start with the man who owns this house."

Tess chuckled. "Handsome, isn't he? I met Walker the day after I arrived in town. He actually helped me move in."

"Why does everyone call him by his last name?" Alex asked, then took a bite of fried chicken.

"I guess it's like a nickname. I'm sad you couldn't have met him when he was always smiling and joking, even though he was a bit of a ladies' man."

"Why the change?"

"Since becoming Cody's guardian, he's reformed his ways. And he's becoming a really good single dad."

Alex searched the room for the man in question and wondered what had happened to the little boy's real father. Their eyes met briefly before he turned away, but she hadn't missed the way he watched her when he thought she wasn't looking. Was he just a cop concerned about a stranger in his home, or did he also feel the spark between them? "With all he has going on, it's no wonder he forgot about renting a room to me."

Tess paused with a bite midway to her mouth. "A room? I thought you were Dr. Clark's niece."

"No, I'm Alex. Months ago, I saw Luke's ad for a room for rent. I plan to be here for a month to recharge before starting my career, and a house with a kitchen seemed a better option than a hotel. But since he no longer lives alone, once a room is available, it'll be hotel life for me after all."

Tess studied Luke a moment and waved when he glanced their way. Her smile widened. "He might discover he likes having another adult in the house."

Luke talked with some of his guests while keeping an observant eye on the intriguing woman who wanted to live under his roof. Alexandra was gorgeous—too gorgeous—in a midthigh floral dress that showed off tanned legs that went on for miles. When she pulled sticks, which looked a lot like paintbrushes, from her hair and her wild, auburn mane tumbled around her shoulders, he had to ask Mr. Grant to repeat his question. This roommate situation was problematic for his plan to change his wild ways.

What were the chances of the woman outside the Acorn Café being his forgotten renter? And what kind of woman showed up in a new town with no car and rented a room in a stranger's home like some wandering hippie? She was obviously too naive to the dangers of the world.

He hadn't been worried about renting a room when it was just him in the house. Now, there was his nephew to consider. Having a stranger temporarily enter their lives was not the stability he'd sworn to provide. But he couldn't kick her out onto the street. After the party—and assuming the call he'd made came back with a clean background check on one Alexandra Roth from Manhattan— he'd let her stay through the holiday weekend and arrange for a room at the hotel after that.

He excused himself at an appropriate moment to check on Cody, and retrieved the empty plate, glad the boy had finally eaten something. "Ready to come out?"

As was often the case since his mother's death, his nephew didn't respond.

Luke settled with his back against the wall beside the front door, and that's when he noticed the guitar and large suitcase. Alexandra must be a musician. She'd been tapping out musical rhythms with Cody. At first, he'd panicked that a stranger was sitting with Cody, but the woman's open demeanor had calmed him. She'd been kind and understanding toward his nephew. His phone dinged with a text message from the police station, and he scanned the information, glad to see his houseguest wasn't a wanted criminal.

The front door opened, and Chief Anson Curry came in with his adopted daughter, Hannah, on his hip. The little girl leaned forward to hug Luke, then wiggled to get down.

"Where Cody?" she asked.

"He's behind the couch. Hey, buddy, Hannah is here. Can you come out, please?"

The little boy crawled out, and the children walked toward Cody's bedroom while Hannah chattered away about her puppy.

Anson's gaze found his wife across the room, and his smile brightened. "Who's the woman Tess is talking to?"

"That would be the roommate I forgot about."

"What? Really?"

"Remember I put out another ad to rent a room and a guy named Alex accepted right before I lost my sister?"

"Dude. That's no guy."

"No kidding, Sherlock."

"Are you trying to recreate my experience of renting my house to Tess and ending up with a wife and daughter?"

"Hell no. I told you I thought she was a guy."

"You thought wrong. Don't you usually run a background check on renters?"

"Always, but the timing on this one sucked." It hadn't been the only thing to fall off his to-do list around the time his sister died. "I called the station. She has a clean record. Not even a traffic violation."

"What are you going to do now?"

"I guess I'll let her stay a few nights until we get it worked out."

Anson's eyes narrowed as he observed her. "She looks safe enough."

The woman in question glanced their way as if sensing their scrutiny. Her eyes rounded as she took in the man in uniform, and then she set aside her empty plate and walked their way.

"Did you call in backup because I've crashed your party?"

"I'm only here as a guest. I'm Anson Curry." He stuck out a hand and they shook. "Welcome to Oak Hollow."

"Pleasure to meet you. I'm Alexandra Charlotte

Roth from New York City. Would you like to see my ID?"

Neither man could hold back their smile.

"Or, I could come down to the station for some fingerprinting and interrogation. In fact, if you have an empty cell, I might need a place to sleep for the night."

Anson laughed. "I don't think we need to go that far."

"Go find your wife," Luke said to Anson, then opened the front door and motioned for Alexandra to step outside. "Let's talk."

He quickly changed his mind about joining her on the porch swing and leaned against the railing, trying to find anywhere to look other than at the striking shade of her green eyes. Normally, he had confidence to spare around women. Why did she make him jumpy as a cat in a room full of rocking chairs? "You can have my bedroom." That's not at all what he'd planned to say, but all the questions flew out of his head.

"I don't expect you to give up your room. I can sleep on the couch tonight and look for something else tomorrow."

"It's no trouble. Cody has bunk beds."

"I appreciate that. Your mother raised you right."

"My sister gets half the credit. You can stay here until a room is available at the hotel. I'll make sure she gives you the one with the efficiency kitchen. And for the same price as you planned to pay here."

She arched an eyebrow. "She owes you?"

"Who?"

"The hotel owner."

He ignored the question. It came with memories he didn't like to talk about, especially today. He crossed one boot over the other and picked at a fleck of peeling paint on the railing. "There's something you need to know if you're going to spend any time here. My nephew isn't like most kids, and he needs things done in a certain way. He requires extra patience and understanding."

"He's on the autism spectrum. Right?"

"Yes." He was surprised she'd recognized it so quickly.

"I was a nanny for a while, and Cody reminds me of one of my kiddos. And my mom is a family-practice doctor. I used to go to work with her during the summer," she explained.

The door opened and Hannah danced out onto the porch, ponytail swinging as she bounced like a pogo stick. "Cake and sing."

"I love cake," Alex said.

Luke watched her hop off the swing like an excited child and follow Hannah inside. He hadn't questioned her as he'd planned, but there was time for that. He stayed in his spot for a few more breaths, preparing himself to smile and act happy when everyone sang "Happy Birthday."

Chapter Three

Once all the party guests had gone, Alex gathered a few stray dishes and carried them into the kitchen. Luke was standing at the sink with his hands on a soapy, half-washed pan, staring into space.

She eased the dirty dishes into the water and propped a hip against the counter. "I think that's the last of it. Why didn't you want to have a party?"

He swung his head and pinned her with an assessing gaze. "Why are you here?"

His abrupt tone startled her, and she stepped back. His obsidian eyes followed her movements, but he remained still, soap bubbles dripping from his fingers. The easygoing, seemingly shy cowboy had once again left the building, and Officer Luke Walker was apparently making his official appearance.

"What made you travel across the country by bus to a small Texas town and rent a room in a stranger's home?"

His brusque, accusatory manner made her edgy, and she hated the feeling. "My mother…" What could she say without giving too much away? If only she hadn't promised to hide her true purpose for this long vacation in Oak Hollow. "She visited and said it was a nice place for some peace and quiet. I need a change of pace and scenery while I work out what direction to take my life."

He dropped the pan into the water, splashing the front of his T-shirt. "Are there that many options?"

"Sure. I believe there are."

"I was twelve when I knew I'd be a police officer."

Her eyebrows sprang toward her hairline. She'd had this conversation before and did not want to hear it from him. "Well, isn't that great for you."

"You really need to be more careful." He crossed his arms over his broad chest like one might do while scolding a naughty child. "Running around the country all by yourself isn't smart."

His judgment made her stomach knot, and her warm feelings for him vanished. "I'm not a child, or some helpless female."

"You *are* female, and you have to be careful and make smart decisions."

Because she needed a place to sleep tonight, she bit her tongue to calm herself before speaking. "You don't know anything about me, my decisions or my life."

"As a cop, I've seen and heard things that I don't even want to repeat, and I know what can happen to women who are irresponsible and reckless."

He did not just call me irresponsible and reckless!

Those were attributes she did not want linked to her. Her ex-boyfriend had called her irresponsible when she hadn't ordered enough wine for the snooty party she hadn't even wanted to plan, but he'd been trying to groom her to be his trophy wife and entertainment coordinator.

"We're done talking. I'll take the couch tonight." Sleeping in his bed was suddenly objectionable. She rushed from the kitchen to gather what she needed from her suitcase and found the adorable little boy cross-legged in front of the TV watching *Mary Poppins*. "I love that movie."

Cody paused the video. "Where's your umbrella?"

She glanced at the television screen and realized he must be referring to Mary Poppins floating down from the sky. "It's in my bag." She picked up her fringed purse and pulled out the collapsible, floral-print umbrella, opened it and twirled it above her head.

"Do you have a kite in there?"

"No. I'm afraid I don't, but we can buy one."

"Okay."

This child was adorable, and he knew how to make her smile. "Do you need to get into the bathroom before I take a shower?"

He swung his head her way and then quickly

shifted his gaze to the ceiling. "No shower! Too much water."

She kneeled beside him, hoping to calm the fear that flashed in his eyes. "I'm not going to make you take a shower, but can I have one?"

"Okay." He sighed and went back to watching his movie.

Dishes still clanged in the kitchen, so she went directly into the hallway bathroom before he decided he had any other advice to dole out. The blue-and-white bathroom was surprisingly neat and organized. Even the towels were perfectly folded and hanging at even levels. Not what you'd expect in an all-male household. Maybe it had just been tidied up for the party?

Hopefully they wouldn't be upset about her somewhat artistic take on housekeeping. She was never dirty. Filth disgusted her, but the rule about "everything in its place" didn't seem necessary. She'd been known to leave art supplies in every room just in case inspiration hit. And sometimes items just needed to be out so you could see them or be reminded of a project that needed doing.

She turned on the water in the shower, stripped and climbed in, desperate to wash away the dust and weariness of travel. Standing under the hot spray helped temper her irritation with Luke, but she still needed to get out of his house as soon as possible. The last thing she wanted was his attitude and judgment messing with her mood. Hopefully, she could get a hotel room the day after the Fourth of July celebration. That left one week that she'd have to deal with Officer Know-it-all.

When she came out of the bathroom in her most modest pajamas, she heard Luke's voice coming from Cody's bedroom next door.

"You have to take a bath, buddy. I'll only put a few inches of water in the tub."

"Promise?"

"Yes. I promise."

She stuck her head into the child's superhero-themed room, also shockingly tidy. "The bathroom is free. Good night."

Sleep wouldn't come until she played around with the melody that had been spiraling in her head, so she sat on the couch with her acoustic guitar. Luke's deep voice carried through the house, coaxing his nephew into the bathtub and telling him how brave he was. She grudgingly admitted that he was good with the kid and continued strumming the new tune.

A few minutes later, Cody peeked around the corner, and she motioned for him to come closer. In a set of Spider-Man pajamas, he sat on the floor in front of her, his eyes intently watching her fingers on the strings.

Luke stood at the edge of the room like a sentinel. After two songs, he moved in to kneel beside his nephew. "It's bedtime."

When the child ignored his uncle, Alex stood and continued playing while she walked to his bedroom, and Cody followed her as if she was the Pied Piper.

She played a soft, slow melody while they moved stuffed animals off the bed and into a row along one wall. She moved into a second song while Luke switched on a race-car night-light, checked under the bed and tucked his nephew under the Batman comforter. One song later, Cody's eyes fluttered closed. She left the room, put away her guitar and curled up on the couch with the quilt she'd pulled off the back of a chair.

She was on the verge of dozing off when Luke cleared his throat.

"If you're not going to take my bed, at least have a pillow."

She took it without saying a word and rolled over to face the back of the couch. His boots shuffled against the wooden floor, and she wondered what he was waiting for.

He cleared his throat again. "Thank you for—for how you are with Cody."

She felt guilty about her childish behavior and turned to see him leave the room, perfectly fitted jeans hugging a very nice butt. "You're welcome," she called after him. She might be mad at the caveman, but her mother raised her to be gracious when someone said "thank you." And due to her current situation, they would have to find a way to coexist.

Luke woke the next morning to the repetition of Cody calling his name. He groaned, but opened his eyes and climbed out of bed, way too early for a Sunday morning, then tracked the disturbance to the hallway bathroom. "What's wrong, buddy? Why are you up so early?"

Cody waved a hand at the disarray of female beauty products across the blue-tiled counter. "Big mess. Big, big mess." He started lining up the bottles and tubes by order of size and shape.

"I'll talk to her about putting her stuff away. Don't break anything." He started to leave the bathroom but turned back. "And don't open any of it."

He needed to speak to Alexandra about keeping things orderly. Probably just one more thing that would make her mad at him. Luke knew his line of questions the night before had upset her, and he'd almost apologized, but having her annoyed with him seemed a good option. If she liked him, it would be way too difficult to resist the crazy attraction and not try to share her bed.

She wasn't on the couch, and the scents of coffee and bacon wafted from the kitchen, making his stomach rumble. A floral-print sundress swung around her legs as she swayed to the beat of an Eagles song on the radio. One strap hung off her shoulder, begging him to kiss the curve of her neck. Feel her softness under his lips. Discover the taste of her skin. He pressed the base of his palms against his eyes. This line of thinking was going to a place he did *not* need to be.

"You're an early riser," he said.

She spun around with a spatula in her hand. "Not normally…" Her eyes rounded and scanned his bare chest. "I couldn't sleep."

He pressed his lips together to keep from smiling. It was hard work keeping in shape, and he appreciated the silent admiration. At least he'd slept in running shorts and hadn't appeared in his normal morning attire of boxers. He poured a cup of coffee, inhaled the blissful aroma and took a sip. It was strong, just the way he liked it.

Great. One more reason to like her.

"I hope it's okay that I'm cooking?" she said, without turning to look at him again.

"Sure."

"I heard Cody yelling. Is everything okay?"

He changed his mind about starting in on her first thing, especially since she was doing a job he disliked. They could discuss house rules after they'd eaten. "He's organizing your makeup and stuff. You might want to check that he doesn't mess anything up."

She shrugged. "It's all replaceable. I'm sorry I didn't put it away. I'm used to having my own bathroom."

"You live alone?"

"I share an apartment with my mom. It's always been just the two of us."

That bit of telling information fit his initial impression that Alexandra Roth wasn't used to a man giving her his opinion.

Cody came into the kitchen and settled into a chair at the table.

"Good morning, Cody." She put bacon, fruit and

an egg casserole on the table. "Let's eat. What do you guys plan to do today?"

"Sunday. Flowers," the little boy said and swiped a piece of bacon.

A pang thudded in Luke's chest. He both loved and hated the day. "Every Sunday we take flowers to the cemetery."

"That's a beautiful tradition." Her hand hovered above Cody's, but he jerked away before she could touch him.

Luke caught her gaze and saw the apology in her eyes. Why did he feel the need to ease her discomfort? "We have a neighbor who lets us cut flowers from her garden."

"How nice of her." She bit into a large strawberry and moaned. "Oh, wow. Yes. So-o-o delicious."

Cody giggled at her dramatic response. And Luke nearly swallowed his tongue.

"What? It's a good strawberry," she said and popped the other half into her mouth.

How would he survive even a few days with her brand of temptation under his roof? "This egg thing you made is good."

"You sound surprised."

He studied the bite on his fork. "Did I have all these ingredients in my refrigerator?"

"I used leftovers from the party. Culinary school taught me a few tricks."

"Is that one of the choices you're considering? Being a chef?"

"It's not off the table, but it's my music-therapy

degree that I really want to use. It's just a question of where and in what capacity."

"Ca-pa-ci-ty," Cody said slowly and then repeated it several times.

"He likes the sound of certain words," Luke explained.

"Me, too. Words are awesome. I think I'll walk around town and explore a bit today. Anywhere particular I should go?"

"Not everything will be open on Sunday, but since you like food and cooking, you should check out the Acorn Café and Bakery. It's on the square."

"I've seen it." She met his gaze and widened her eyes. "Yesterday. I was standing right outside the door when *someone* rushed out like his boots were on fire."

"Oh, yeah. Sorry about almost crashing into you. You should go inside this time. Sam Hargrove is a great cook."

"Hargrove?" Her fork clattered onto her plate.

Cody covered his ears and squeezed his eyes shut. "Too loud."

"Yes," Luke said slowly. "Does that name mean something to you?"

"Just like the sound of it." Her eyes shifted down and to the left, and her knee bounced rapidly.

And he knew she was lying. "Try not to get yourself into any trouble today."

The tight-lipped glare she pinned on him was enough to undo the pleasant mood they'd shared over breakfast. A tingle of guilt lodged uncomfortably in his chest, but riling her up was the only way he knew to keep her at a necessary distance. On second thought, not so much distance that he couldn't keep a watchful eye and discover her secrets.

Was she hiding from someone? Running away? Was she in danger?

Even with suspicions, his protective instincts fired to life.

Chapter Four

A pleasant breeze rustled the trees, and it was early enough that the thermometer hadn't spiked. Alex stood on the front porch of her very temporary dwelling and waved goodbye to Cody as the guys went down the steps, but when Luke glanced over his shoulder, she only raised an eyebrow. "Try not to get into trouble," she mumbled to herself in her best imitation of his Southern drawl. His high-handed request goaded the part of her that couldn't resist a dare, but focusing too much attention on sparring with Luke could jeopardize her reason for being here.

She leaned across the porch railing to get a better look at Luke and Cody ambling side by side down the shady sidewalk, and she couldn't resist pulling her phone from her fringed bag and taking their picture. Matching boots, same brand of jeans and similar strides. It was like watching young and old versions of the same person. The swing of Cody's arms and the slight drag of one heel matched his uncle's. She giggled when they both shoved a hand in their back left pocket at the same moment. Had Cody watched his uncle Luke and tried to copy his swagger, or was it genetic? Was there anyone in this town who walked like her, or shared her belief that ginger tastes like soap?

Alex adjusted her wide-brimmed hat and set off in the opposite direction of the cowboy and his Mini-Me. Following them to the cemetery felt like an intrusion on their pain. Later this evening, when the light was just right, she'd go alone and find her father's grave.

When she'd awakened at dawn, she had prepared to put on a happy face and get through a few days with a man who was doing his best to bring out the feisty female inside her. But she had not been ready for him to appear half-dressed, with sexy, bedhead hair and a hint of self-assured strutting. She suspected the "ladies' man" that Tess Curry mentioned was fighting to come out and seduce her. No doubt, Luke had plans to set her on a straight-and-narrow path leading to a safe, responsible career, but his brand of sanctimonious preaching wasn't something she needed. She and her mother had done just fine over the years without anyone else telling them what to do.

Her free-spirited mother had always encouraged exploration of life and opportunities, starting with Alex's childhood modeling career. Seven years in that industry, and smart investments on her mother's part, had earned her a nest egg that helped fund culinary school, art classes and finally a music-therapy degree. Taking care of herself had never been a problem.

She trailed her fingers along the top of a low stone wall, and a brown rabbit sprang from beneath a flowering bush, making her yelp and then laugh. Some of her Luke-induced irritation bounded away with the bunny. She backtracked her walk from the previous evening and returned to the town square. Red, white and blue swags decorated the historic buildings, and a young couple was stringing star-shaped lights on the gazebo. Her eyes went straight to the Acorn Café's circular metal-and-wood, tree-of-life sign. She rubbed the spot high on her hip where a tree-of-life tattoo decorated her skin. Maybe she wasn't the only one in the family who was drawn to the image.

When she'd mentioned culinary school to Luke, dread had struck that she was in for another lecture on the consequences of still not knowing what she wanted to do with her life, but at least the mention of cooking had yielded information she was looking for. She could've defended herself by talking about her job interview for a music-therapist position at the prestigious Carrington Clinic in Manhattan. It had gone well, but she didn't have the experience to actually get the job and doubted she'd hear back from them.

Unsure how to go about her amateur detective work, she sat on a wrought-iron bench and admonished herself for not doing more research before leaving New York. She'd wanted the thrill of a firsthand experience, but this adventure was proving to be more difficult than expected. She reviewed the mental list of things she knew from her mother's stories. Her grandparents, William and Audrey Hargrove, had both lived their entire lives in this town. William had his own law practice and was a member of the city council. Her father's younger brother, Sam, was a good athlete and had idolized his older brother.

Alex stood to go into the café but worried it might seem weird if she sat in a restaurant not eating, so she set off to explore and work up an appetite. How much had the town changed since her father lived here? Would she find some trace of the mark he'd left on his hometown? Renewed excitement about her search quickened her steps.

Most of the shops on the square were closed or wouldn't open for another thirty minutes, but she enjoyed window-shopping and brief conversations with several people. The citizens of this small town were very welcoming. More so than her irksome landlord. One minute he was friendly, and the next he pushed her buttons, almost as if he enjoyed irritating her.

She peered into the window of a vintage clothing shop that promised treasures that would require a second suitcase on her return trip. Mannequins and racks displayed styles ranging from the 1930s to the 1970s. An emerald-green dress with a bustier-style top caught her eye, and she wondered what Luke would think of it.

Damn! Why does he keep invading my thoughts?

The lock clicked, and a young woman opened the door. "Good morning. Come on inside and look around. I'm just unpacking a few boxes of new merchandise, and I can tell by your style that you'll find some items you'll love."

"I think you might be right." Alex stepped into the cool, colorful space, scented with something lightly spicy and a hint of fresh-baked cookies. "You have a great shop."

"It belongs to my grandmother. I help out in the summer when I'm not teaching kindergarten. I'm Emma, by the way."

"Nice to meet you. I'm Alex. You teach here in Oak Hollow?"

"Yes. Born and raised here and can't seem to escape." Emma sighed and hung up a long black dress. "I teach at the same elementary where I went to school."

"Do you have a student named Cody? I'm staying with him and his uncle Luke until a hotel room becomes available."

Emma looked momentarily confused. "Oh, Walker. I'm not used to hearing him called by his first name. Cody will be in my class this coming school year."

"Is it a cop thing to go by your last name?"

"It goes back to his high-school-football days. Star quarterback and town hero when they won the championship."

That information fit with Luke's somewhat macho attitude. "So you've known him a long time?"

"Most of my life. His sister used to babysit me."

Alex almost asked about Cody's father and how Luke had ended up as guardian, but asking a stranger seemed too invasive. She tucked away her questions for later, looked through every rack and tried on a stack of clothes while they continued to chat. An hour later, she left with the emerald dress, a pair of brown leather sandals, a perfectly worn denim jacket and a blue-and-white polka dot dress for the Fourth of July picnic.

After walking around the square twice to build up her courage—and temper her expectations—she stepped into the Acorn Café. The smell of freshly baked bread made her mouth water, and breakfast seemed a distant memory. It was early for lunch and only a few tables were occupied, but she took a seat at the counter, where she could see the cook through the serving window. The man looked to be in his midforties and had short blond hair and broad shoulders that made him look more like a linebacker than a chef.

He caught her staring and flashed a dimpled smile. "Someone will be right with you."

The man went back to work, singing in a deep baritone voice along with the radio that was faintly playing in the kitchen. Had her singing talent come from her father's family? Because it sure hadn't come from her mother. She shook her head, trying not to get carried away. There was no guarantee this man was a relative.

She picked up a menu with her paternal family name in big, bold letters across the top. Underneath was a black-and-white version of the tree of life from their front sign. She had the urge to dig out the set of watercolors from her purse and add a bit of color and life to the artwork.

A waitress rushed out of the swinging kitchen door. "Sorry for the wait. What can I get for you?"

"I'd love to start with a Coke."

"You got it."

"I've heard the food is really good here. Who's cooking today?"

The young girl hitched a thumb over her shoulder. "The owner. Sam Hargrove."

Her pulse picked up speed and she couldn't keep the smile from her face. Her father's brother. Her uncle. For the first time, she was laying eyes on the part of her family she only knew from her mother's stories and a few old photos. She was so engrossed in searching his face for hints of her own, she missed what the waitress said. "Sorry, what did you ask me?"

"Do you know what you want to eat, or would you like a few more minutes to decide?"

"I'll have a cheeseburger with no onions, please."

"Fries?"

"Definitely. And a glass of water with no ice."

The waitress wrote up the order, clipped it onto a cord strung across the opening to the kitchen and served her a Coke and a water.

While Alex waited—and to keep from looking like a lunatic staring at her uncle—she slid the front page out of the menu's protective sleeve, got out her travel set of watercolors and started painting. When a plate covered with golden fries and a tall burger appeared in front of her, she looked up to see her uncle Sam standing before her and eyeing her artwork.

"I'm sorry," she said quickly. "I should've asked before I ruined one of your menus."

"Don't apologize. I'd say it's quite the improvement. Much better than the crayon art the children do on the kids menus."

Alex laughed, relaxed by his easygoing manner. "I'm glad to hear art classes are paying off."

He cocked his head and studied her. "Are you from around here? You look familiar."

"No. I'm from…" Nerves jumped in her stomach. "From the east coast. Just visiting. People have said I look like the actress Jessica Chastain. Maybe that's why I look familiar?"

"Could be. Enjoy your burger." He slid a bottle of ketchup closer and headed back into the kitchen.

The fries were crisp, perfectly salted and made her taste buds very happy. As the café began to fill up with the after-church lunch crowd, she listened in on the conversations she could hear and searched every face, hoping another piece of important information might be revealed.

* * *

Cody placed the bouquet of handpicked flowers on the very center of his mother's grave and then did his usual three-circle walk around the plot before settling cross-legged at the foot. He arranged a row of pebbles along the top of the limestone border they'd constructed a few weeks ago.

Luke pulled a dandelion from the edge of his sister's gravestone and wiped dry crumbles of dirt from his hands. It was surprisingly pleasant under the shade of the big old oak tree, and even though they never stayed for long, it would be nice to have somewhere to sit. Building a bench would be their next project. Finding ways to connect with Cody, and letting him know how much he loved him, were his top priorities. Not gorgeous redheads. He moved to his parents' graves, brushed fallen leaves from their shared stone and sent up a silent prayer that he was worthy of raising his nephew.

"What should we have for lunch?" Luke asked.

"Acorn Café."

"Sounds good." *Maybe she'll be there.* He cursed under his breath. Why couldn't he keep his mind from straying back to Alexandra?

Cody crouched beside the headstone as he did every Sunday before they left the cemetery. Luke had been wondering what he always said, and this time, he moved close enough to hear what his nephew whispered.

"Did you send my new mommy yet? I'm being a good boy. I love you."

A slash of sorrow caught in Luke's throat, making it difficult to even breathe. His nephew was waiting and hoping for a new mommy. And it was up to him to find her. To find a wife that would be stable, understanding, patient, loving and all the things this special little boy needed. What was he supposed to do with this piece of information? Run out and order up a mail-order bride?

Fine. He'd start dating again, but it could only be with women who were right for the job. Not his usual shallow party girls. And someone with more self-awareness and stability than the wandering woman who'd appeared on his doorstep. Someone who'd be happy in his small town.

The hopeful little boy pulled one flower out of the bouquet and walked toward the gate.

"Wait up. Let's go home and get the truck. I need to run an errand before we eat."

Cody nodded and studied a ladybug crawling on the yellow blossom he held tightly in his little hands.

When they got home, Cody went straight to the large collegiate volume of the dictionary, carefully opened it past the other pages filled with dried blossoms and pressed the newest edition between the pages. The hardcover book bulged with its collection from his mother's grave.

The hollow place inside Luke's chest ached, but he didn't know how to fill it. He couldn't stop himself from worrying about Cody missing his mom, but he appeared in good spirits today. Better than most, and Dr. Clark claimed he was doing remarkably well considering everything. If preserving flowers from his mother's grave made his nephew feel better, that was fine with him. He could always buy more books.

Thoughts of the elderly town doctor reminded him of their conversation about his niece, Gwen, who was moving to town to join his medical practice. Dr. Clark wanted to set them up, convinced they'd hit it off. Maybe he'd better consider a date with the quiet, shy nurse practitioner after all.

Once they'd finished their errands, Luke held the door of the Acorn Café while a family of three filed out, and then he swore silently. His temptation sat at the counter with a pile of shopping bags at her feet, her red hair tumbling around her shoulders like a fairy ready to frolic in the woods.

Frolic? Why the hell did that word pop into my head?

It had to be from all the bedtime stories he'd been reading. He glanced around as if someone could hear his ridiculous thoughts, then veered toward their usual two-person table near the front windows.

Cody didn't follow. He headed straight toward Alexandra and climbed up onto the stool beside her, little boots swinging in opposite directions on each side of the metal post.

Why was his shy nephew taking such an unusual liking to this mysterious stranger? Luke rubbed the sudden tension in his neck.

"Hey there, Cody." Alexandra patted his back,

and when he stiffened, she tucked her hand under her thigh. "I bet you're hungry."

Luke caught her eye and watched her beautiful, broad smile fade into... Was her expression contempt...or lust? His blood suddenly ran a little hotter. If things continued like this, he was in trouble. Big trouble. His old dating tendencies—to play the field and be serious about no one—were too close to the surface, and Alexandra was making it a challenge to keep his promise to his sister. His promise to be a better man. Cody came first. He would not go back to juggling a different woman each weekend.

He joined them at the counter and took the empty seat on the other side of his nephew. "How's your morning been?" he asked Alexandra.

"Great. And I haven't caused a bit of trouble... yet."

There was no way he could miss the mischievous grin she attempted to hide. The one that made him want to use his tongue to soothe the indention her teeth pressed into her full lower lip. He had to do something to get her out of his head. So he did the only thing he could think of and set out to continue aggravating her. "Other than painting property that doesn't belong to you?" He reached past Cody and picked up the tree she'd painted and had to admit she was talented.

"Don't mess that up, Walker," Sam called from the kitchen. "I want to show it to my wife and see about getting this young lady's permission to make color copies."

"You have my permission," she said and turned a smug grin on Luke. "See. No trouble. Just spreading joy everywhere I go."

And no doubt breaking hearts. He glanced at her nearly empty plate. "What did you think of the food?"

"Really delicious. I'm stuffed."

"Stuffed," Cody said and tapped the edge of the counter with two fingers. "Stuffed, stuffed, stuffed."

Without even asking, the waitress appeared with iced tea and apple juice. "Afternoon, boys. What else can I get for you?"

"Chicken-fried steak for me, please," Luke said. "And a chicken strip basket for Cody."

"Good choices." She wrote down the order and winked at the little boy.

Alex pulled two more tree drawings from menus, gave one to Cody, along with a second brush, and slid the paints closer. "Dip your brush into the water then swirl it around on the color you like. That's it. Just like that. Purple is a good choice." She coated her brush with the same color and demonstrated brushstrokes.

With Cody not being much for conversation, and him and Alex playing this weird game of spar and retreat, the meal was mostly silent.

When they stood to leave, someone squeezed

Luke's shoulder, and he turned to the owner's mother. "Good afternoon, Mrs. Hargrove."

Alex gasped, dropped her shopping bags and quickly bent to retrieve them.

He tried to see her expression, but she wouldn't look up. This was the second time she'd reacted to the name *Hargrove*.

Sam's mother rubbed his back like he'd seen her do to the men of her family. "Walker, when are you and Cody going to come over for supper?"

"You name the night and we'll be there," he said.

"Excellent. We have a family dinner every Thursday evening."

"Perfect. I hope it's okay if we bring our house guest, Alexandra?"

"Of course." Mrs. Hargrove glanced between them, and her smile grew. "We'd love to have your *friend* join us."

Luke picked up on her not-so-subtle emphasis on the word *friend*. And he was surprised when Alexandra—who usually had plenty to say—remained silent and looked as if she'd seen a ghost, proving his suspicions were warranted.

There was something more to Alexandra Roth's trip to Oak Hollow than she was letting on.

Chapter Five

Alex's mind zinged in a million different directions, and when the café appeared to be tilting, she gripped the edge of the lunch counter. The grandmother she'd never met was standing right in front of her with an open, friendly smile.

"I'm Audrey Hargrove, and we'd be happy for you to join us for supper."

Alex accepted her outstretched hand, her own trembling when their fingers touched. "It's…" Her voice cracked, and she cleared her throat and tried again. "It's a pleasure to meet you."

And so much more emotional than you could ever know.

Audrey squinted and studied Alex from behind green eyes and thick glasses. "Lovely red hair. Believe it or not, I had hair almost that color once upon a time. But I don't have your lovely curls." She smoothed her shiny, gray bob with well-manicured, pale pink nails. "Did you get it from your mother or father?"

"My mother." *And apparently you, as well.* Could this seemingly nice woman be the same one who hadn't approved of her mom, Kate? The woman who'd made it known that her son should marry the local girl he'd dated through most of high school? The woman whose unwelcoming attitude, words and actions had prevented her from knowing she was a grandmother?

"See you all at six on Thursday." Audrey waved to Cody and then rounded the counter and went through the swinging kitchen door.

"Are you okay?" Luke asked and adjusted his tan cowboy hat.

"Yes." She'd squeezed the word past her tight throat. "All good." His observant, dark-eyed gaze bore into her like he could unearth all her secrets, and his throaty grumble implied he didn't believe her claim.

I need to get a grip, or I'm going to blow everything. Because of the way her mother had been treated, she'd expected her grandmother to be a bit on the cold side, but she'd been pleasantly surprised by her friendly nature.

"I'll give you and all of your shopping bags a ride back to the house." Luke motioned for her to lead the way out the door.

She resisted one last glance toward the kitchen and made her way out into the midday sun. It took a moment to adjust to the brightness, and she stood there in a bit of a daze.

Cody held his tree painting in one hand and grabbed hold of a corner of her shopping bag with the other. "Look left. Look right," he said and led her across the street to a row of parking spots near the courthouse.

After several failed attempts to buckle her seat belt, it clicked into place, and she focused on a moth flitting about, just like her mind. The fingernails digging into her palms confirmed the breathing technique she'd learned in yoga class was working about as well as her questionable ability to meet family members…and not reveal her identity. The moment she'd touched her grandmother's hand, she'd wanted to shout out who she was. The experience had been considerably more emotional than anticipated. She would call her mother and try once again to convince her it wouldn't be the end of the world if they told the truth.

"What is it about that family that has you so interested? And jumpy?" Luke shifted into Reverse and backed out of the parking spot.

His questions pulled her from spinning thoughts. "What family?" She kept her eyes fixed on the world outside her window, going on as if nothing had changed.

"The Hargrove family."

"I don't know what you mean." She was in no

mood for an interrogation and needed to shift the conversation to a safe topic. "Is there a nursery or garden center in town?"

He hit the brakes at the stop sign. "Why? Need to buy flowers for someone?"

"For your house." *Not that you deserve it!* "I know I'll only be staying with you for a little while, but would it be okay if I work in your yard?"

"You want to do my yardwork? I really can't picture you pushing a lawn mower. You'd probably mow my grass into some kind of weird designs."

She gritted her teeth and glanced his way, refusing to let his comments get to her. But she couldn't resist admiring his long, tanned arm stretched out to grip the steering wheel. The lines of his muscles were beautifully carved and it looked as if he knew how to hold a girl…and make her feel like a woman. "I was only thinking about planting a few flowers and herbs. Nothing drastic. Just a bit of color and shape."

"Why would you want to work out in the heat and dirt on your vacation?"

"I don't have a yard at home and…" She huffed out a breath and waved a hand as if it could clear away all that was wrong with her situation. Her will to argue with this exasperating—and way too tempting—man disappeared. "Never mind. It was a stupid idea."

He glanced in the rearview mirror and caught his nephew's eye. "Cody, do you think we need flowers in our yard?"

"Yes. Flowers," the young boy said. "Like Nan."

"Who is Nan?" she asked.

"Chief Curry's grandmother. Cody goes over to her house while I work. Either Tess or Hannah's babysitter, Jenny, watches both kids." Luke pulled into the empty parking lot of Oak Hollow Elementary School, made a wide U-turn and headed back in the direction they'd just come.

"Where are we going?"

"To Green Forest Nursery. It's owned by the family of one of my high-school buddies. Might as well get it done today while I'm not working."

Alex tucked one leg under the other and studied his strong profile, her suspicion growing that he was deliberately trying to aggravate her. But why? Of course, not every man she'd been interested in fell at her feet with roses in hand, but Luke's reaction to her sometimes felt unnecessarily aversive. He sure wasn't a fan of hers, and that stung.

There was a nice guy somewhere under his prickliness. She'd caught glimpses of that man in the way he took care of his nephew, and the way he was respected and loved by his friends and the community had been obvious at his birthday party. Could his behavior be a defense?

"No! Not that," Cody wailed and kicked the back of the seat in a rhythmic thumping.

Luke changed the radio station. "He hates that song. Says the beat isn't right. Is this one okay, buddy?"

"Okay. Yes, okay."

"You're really good with him," she said in a tone only Luke could hear.

He shrugged his broad shoulders and pulled into a gravel parking lot. "I try."

"I promise I won't embarrass you with landscaping that's too unusual."

His solemn expression turned into a lopsided grin. "I'll hold you to it."

The family-owned nursery was on the outskirts of town and was framed by a backdrop of rolling hills. Billowy white clouds covered half of the blue dome of sky, and Alex wanted to lie on her back in a patch of grass and watch the cloud shapes morph from one picture to the next. She hopped down from the tall truck and turned toward a field of yellow flowers in the distance. "What are all of those white boxes over there?"

Luke looked where she pointed. "Bee boxes. The neighbor has a honey farm."

"Can we buy some honey?"

"They're closed today, but when they're open you can buy a lot more than honey. They have all kinds of homemade food and beauty products."

Luke rushed to catch up with his eager nephew as they entered the nursery. "Wait up."

Cody insisted on pulling the flatbed cart up and down the aisles of plants as they shopped, and then adjusted every pot into what he deemed the correct position before another could be added. "All done," he finally announced and pulled the load to the front.

The salesgirl rang up their merchandise and announced the total.

Luke dug out his wallet, but Alex motioned for him to put it away. "This was my idea and I'd like to pay for it."

"If you spend all of your money, you won't have any for your bus fare home and might be stuck in Oak Hollow. We wouldn't want that."

The salesgirl shot him a startled, disapproving glance. "Who put a bee in your bonnet, Walker?"

Alex chuckled, smiled at him as sweetly as she could and then handed over her credit card. "While I appreciate your concern, I've got it handled. And by the way, I only rode the bus from the airport in San Antonio. I promise you won't be stuck with me forever. I'll be out of your hair the moment a hotel room becomes available."

Luke winced, ashamed of the way he was talking to her. Why did her statement strike disappointment inside him? The thought of her leaving suddenly made him want to make sure no hotel room ever became available. He got Cody settled in the back seat and started the air conditioner before they loaded the plants into the truck bed. Finally climbing into the cool air of the truck cab was a welcome relief.

"Uncle Luke, music, please."

He tuned the radio to Cody's favorite country station and adjusted an air vent to blow on his face. Alexandra was quiet the whole ride home, and he worried he'd pushed her a bit too far. His plan to keep her at a distance seemed to be working re-markably well. Possibly too well.

He pulled into his driveway, and barely had the engine off before Alexandra fired open her door, lowered the tailgate and started unloading the plants.

Cody held his tree-of-life painting with both hands and jumped down from the running board.

"We'll put your artwork on the refrigerator," Luke said.

Alexandra dropped a pot of basil back onto the tailgate and snapped her fingers. "I've got it." She ran toward the front door.

"Where are you going?" Luke called after her. "What about your shopping bags? And the plants?"

"In a minute. Have to write something down before I forget." She used the key he'd given her and disappeared into the house as the screen door slammed, but she left the wooden door standing wide open.

Luke made a silly face while circling a finger around the side of his head, and Cody giggled. They followed her inside and Luke tripped over the shoes she'd kicked off right inside the doorway. The purse she had been wearing across her body was on the floor a few feet away.

She paced the room with a paisley-print notebook, furiously writing with a hot-pink pen. "That's not right," she mumbled, then ripped out a page, balled it up and tossed it over her shoulder. It bounced off the coffee table and rolled toward the TV.

"Oh, no," Cody said and covered his eyes. "Big mess. Big mess. Big mess."

Luke got a tub of colored blocks and three plastic bowls out of the entertainment-stand drawer and put them on the coffee table. "Here you go, buddy. Sit down and sort these while I talk to Alexandra." He picked up the wadded paper.

She paused midstride, seeming to notice them for the first time, and glanced at the discarded trash in Luke's hand. She bit her lip and scrunched her nose. "Sorry. When I get an idea, I have to write it down before it disappears."

"I see." He'd known quirky artistic types before, and she was definitely one of them. Thankfully, Cody hadn't gone into a meltdown and was totally focused on his sorting job and not paying any attention to the adults. "Sorting things helps calm him down. He likes things in their proper place," Luke said, answering her unasked question.

"I'm so sorry. I'll keep that in mind. I tend to be a bit of a free spirit with my things." She rushed over to pick up her purse and shoes.

"Do you do this in your mother's home?"

She stood up ramrod-straight and looked as if she might throw her shoes at his face, and then she very methodically placed them next to her suitcase and went out the front door with her notebook in hand.

That was a stupid thing to say! Guilt clenched his gut. Why couldn't he seem to resist goading her? Being hurtful was not what he'd intended.

"Uncle Luke, video?"

"You can watch for a few minutes, then take a break to play with your toy cars or a puzzle." He set the timer that always sat on the coffee table.

Cody turned on the television and slid the old videotape of *Mary Poppins* into the VCR—the same one his sister had played for him when he was his nephew's age. A pang of nostalgia and sadness slammed his chest. The pain of losing Libby had been easing recently, but at the moment, he missed her terribly.

The familiar slow and steady creaking of the porch swing drew Luke toward the front windows, and his chest tightened for a whole different reason.

Alexandra sat stretched out on the swing with one long leg across the wooden seat while the other hung down and pushed rhythmically against the painted concrete floor. With her pen tapping the paper, she sang a few lines, then shook her head and ripped out another page. "That's not right, either."

A shiver worked along his spine. He wished she'd go back to singing, because her voice was beautiful, but he moved away from the windows before he got caught gawking. Luke hung his hat on the coatrack, then grabbed her suitcase and guitar from the corner and moved all her belongings into his bedroom. He wouldn't ask her to sleep on the couch again tonight.

On his way back to the living room, he paused at Cody's bedroom door. Considering his height, sleeping on that bunk bed was going to be a challenge, and the couch wasn't any longer. He sighed and rubbed his lower back as just the thought of sleeping on the floor sent phantom pains through his muscles, but a sleeping bag might be his best option. He'd figure that out later.

"Cody, if you need me, I'll be outside unloading the plants." He got no answer. "Give me a sign if you hear me, please."

Cody gave a thumbs-up but never took his eyes from the penguins dancing with Mary Poppins on the TV screen.

Luke watched him a moment longer, but the memories of his own childhood were coming too hard and fast, were too close to the surface. He turned the glass doorknob but waited a beat before opening it to join her outside.

She met his gaze and her eyes shot daggers in his direction. "It's not my mother's apartment. We paid for it jointly and own it equally."

"I see." The disgruntled look on her face made him want to laugh, but he didn't dare. Self-preservation was too strong. He had an idea what prices were like in New York City and wondered where she'd gotten the money for such a purchase, but again, he had enough sense to know that asking was a one-way ticket to the doghouse. "I didn't mean to offend you or interrupt your writing." He took the stairs two at a time and was only halfway down the front walk before she caught up to him.

"You should go inside and tend to Cody. I'll unload the plants. Getting them was my idea. And some of them are for the backyard."

"Won't take but a minute, and Cody is well entertained by his movie."

"You shouldn't let him watch too much TV."

"Thanks for the parenting tip, but it seems I've heard that tidbit of information somewhere before."

She mumbled something under her breath and shot him a sideways glance.

Is this really the way I want things to be between us? Constant sparring?

They were getting along about as well as feral cats fighting over territory. He'd ease up on the annoying comments.

They worked in silence while unloading the pots of rosemary, basil, lemon balm and lavender, along with trays of colorful flowers. He set plants in a random cluster at the edge of the porch, but she stood back and surveyed before placing each pot in a specific spot in the flower beds.

Just as he moved in to get a closer look, she stepped backward. Her body—and nicely rounded bottom—collided with the front of his, and he clasped her hips to keep her from pitching forward. Lust hit him like a sledgehammer, and he tipped his head to smell her hair. If he swept her curls to the side, he could press his lips to the soft skin of her neck…and see if she tasted as good as she smelled.

Chapter Six

Alex stood perfectly still, not wanting to interrupt the unexpected physical connection with Luke. The hard press of his body against the length of hers, strong hands clutching her hips, warm breath against her ear. All the sensations swirled together, and she shivered as a fire lit in her core. She risked leaning back a little more to rest her weight against him, seeking the comfort she craved.

Cody fired open the screen door, and Luke pulled away like she'd scalded him, but thankfully he braced his hands on her shoulders when she listed backward.

"Ding, ding, ding. Timer rang," the young boy said, then went back inside.

Luke crossed to the other side of the walkway. "Sorry."

What's he sorry for? Almost making me melt with desire or jerking away like I'm rubbish?

Embarrassment flushed her skin. Had the moment she'd believed was mutual attraction only been one-sided and all in her head? Had she lingered against him for a moment too long and revealed a yearning he didn't reciprocate?

Face it. I'm not his type.

"Don't let me keep you from what you normally do on a Sunday. I got this," she said in her best attempt at nonchalance, praying he didn't know what his rejection was doing to her. Alex rushed to his truck and got the last tray of daisies. When she returned to the flower bed, he was nowhere to be seen.

After placing each pot where she thought it should be planted, she didn't have the will or energy to dig holes. And she didn't want to see Luke to ask for the garden tools. Alex once again settled on the swing with her notebook and went back to writing her song about what makes a family. And now, she also had an idea for a sad song of unrequited love.

A few hours later, Cody joined her on the porch, handed her an Oreo cookie, and then held a finger to his lips and made a shushing sound.

"Thank you," she whispered. "This is exactly what I needed."

He settled on the top step and bit into his own treat.

The lowering sunlight glinted off his dark hair

and made her want to stroke his head and cuddle him on her lap to ease the sadness in his eyes, but she knew her touch would not be welcomed by this little guy any more than it was by his uncle.

"Spaghetti okay for supper?"

Luke's voice startled her, and half of her cookie dropped onto her lap. "Sounds good. I love spaghetti."

"Don't get too excited. It's just a jar of sauce from the grocery." His eyes narrowed. "Where'd you get the cookie?"

"Ummm." If she admitted the truth, would Cody be in trouble for getting into the snacks?

"Cody Walker, have you been in the cookie jar this close to supper?"

The little boy turned around, chocolate smeared around his mouth and cheeks, which were puffed out like a chipmunk hiding his stash of nuts. He shook his head from side to side.

Luke ducked his head to hide a smile. "You might want to wash your face, kiddo."

Alex gathered up the wadded paper she'd strewn across the swing. "I can help you. I have a few ideas for spicing things up." The second the words left her mouth, his big, dark eyes flared like he could see right into her fantasies. "The jar of sauce," she clarified quickly. "I'll help cook."

"Spicy is good," he said around a devil's grin and restrained laughter. "I'd like the help. Cody, do not leave the front yard." Luke opened the screen door and paused like he'd say something more, but then turned and went back into the house.

Butterflies danced in her belly. Nothing was more frustrating than a man sending mixed signals.

Should I go in alone and see if he's hinting at more?

She smacked her forehead with the palm of her hand, instantly dismissing that terrible idea. And after misreading his intentions earlier, it would be best not to go inside alone. The last thing she wanted to do was embarrass herself again. "Want to help with dinner?" she asked her cookie companion.

The little boy stood and quietly followed her inside.

The first thing Alex noticed was the empty spot where her suitcase and guitar had been. "Go wash your face like your uncle asked, and I'll meet you in the kitchen." After scanning the room and still not seeing her belongings, she ventured down the hallway and finally found them in Luke's bedroom at the back of the house. Her suitcase was on a wooden trunk at the foot of his bed, her guitar propped in the corner and a stack of folded towels sat on the bed.

Alex flopped back onto Luke's navy-and-gray bedspread—the bed had been made with tight corners she'd be lucky to duplicate in the morning—and stared at the ceiling. She'd accept his offer to use his bedroom, but with his cedar-and-musk scent infusing the air, she couldn't stop thinking about things she shouldn't. His lips caressing the skin on the back of her neck. Turning into his arms for a teasing first kiss. A night of long, slow…

Stop it! How will I get any rest with that vision of him in nothing but a pair of running shorts at breakfast?

The sudden recollection of his comments about her irresponsible ways was the splash of reality needed to pull her from her fantasies. His opinions were not qualities she was looking for in a partner.

She rolled onto her stomach and propped her chin on her hands. His space was sparsely decorated and, of course, neat as a pin. A photo of Luke, Cody and a woman who looked a lot like them sat on the dresser next to a plaster cast of a child's hand. Under the bedside table lamp were a notepad, a pen and a tattered detective novel with a leather bookmark. A floorboard creaked behind her, and she jerked around to see Luke leaning casually against the door frame. "You seem to have a knack for sneaking up on me."

He arched a dark eyebrow. "Hiding something?"

"No." She bit her tongue. That one word had come out sounding more like a question than a statement. "Cody is waiting in the kitchen to help make dinner." She climbed off the bed but caught sight of the upturned corners of his full, tempting mouth. At least Luke wasn't glaring at her suspiciously.

"You can use my room until the hotel has a vacancy. I just need to grab a few things for the morning." He opened the closet and pulled out his Oak Hollow police uniform.

Oy vey! I bet he looks really hot in that uniform.

Alex slipped out of the room to give him privacy, and because being alone with him next to a bed only increased her longing for a perplexing man who did not return her feelings. His hot-and-cold attitude was beyond confusing. When she made it into the kitchen, Cody was walking in circles around the table.

"Sorry it took me so long, little man. Let's get out all of our ingredients and start cooking."

"Ingredients?" he said and then repeated it slowly while tapping out the number of syllables.

"That means everything we need to mix together to make the food."

"Do we need a spoonful of sugar?" he asked in a hopeful tone.

The Mary Poppins reference made her chuckle. "I think we do."

Luke joined them in the kitchen and was more in the way than he was helpful, but Cody seemed so happy, she wasn't about to tell him they didn't need his assistance.

"Why are you putting sugar on the pasta?" he asked his nephew.

"Because, Uncle Luke, a spoonful of sugar helps you take your medicine."

Luke looked momentarily perplexed, then chuckled and shared a smile with Alex.

"Everything is ready. Let's sit down and eat."

She put the bread in the center of the table and took her seat.

"Uncle Luke, we need a kite. She doesn't have one in her bag."

"That's easy enough," he said. "We can get one sometime this week."

"And I need a piano," Cody said before stuffing a large bite of spaghetti into his mouth.

"You do? That might be a little harder to get, but I have an old electronic keyboard under my bed. Want to start with that?"

"Okay," Cody mumbled around his mouthful of food.

Alex was thoroughly enjoying the interaction between them. "I play the piano. Do you want me to teach you a few things?"

"Yes. You teach me," the little boy said.

By the time they'd finished a lengthy conversation about the kitten that Cody wanted, and his uncle did not, they were full and laughing.

"It's bath time," Luke said. "Go pick out the pajamas you want to wear tonight."

Alex glanced at the darkening sky outside the kitchen window. It was too late to find her father's grave tonight. "Luke, how do I get to the cemetery? I wanted to go this morning, but I didn't want to interrupt your visit."

His brow scrunched, and he waited a few beats before speaking. "Go straight up the street in the opposite direction from the square and then left on Cypress Creek. You'll run right into it. Why do you—"

"I like to visit cemeteries in different parts of the country," she interrupted, not wanting to hear his next question. One that could lead to things she'd have to keep hidden, and she was a terrible liar. "You should see the burying grounds in Boston. There's always something to sketch." Her statement was true, and he didn't need to hear the main reason she was so determined to see this particular cemetery.

He shrugged and grabbed his glass of iced tea on the way out of the room.

While they were busy with bath time, she went out into the backyard to call her mother, but before she could pull up her contacts, the sights and sounds of the night engulfed her. The lawn mowers, children's laughter and other sounds of the day had faded into the nocturnal music of chirping crickets, wind in the trees, the hoot of an owl and something she couldn't identify that rose and fell in volume. It was a symphony that needed no words.

After a few minutes of holding perfectly still to let nature calm her, she walked toward the double hammock in the corner of the large yard. Her bare feet sunk into thick grass that tickled her toes with each step and made her want to dance under the moonlight and around the large oak tree. It had a knothole on the trunk and elegantly arching branches, much like the tattoo she'd designed. It was the kind of tree that she imagined housed magical creatures, and she decided to name it Fairy Oak.

Stretching out on the green-and-white-striped hammock, Alex gazed at the sky. It was a clear evening and an amazing array of stars were twinkling to life. She took her eyes off the view long enough to dial her mom's number.

Kate answered after two rings. "Hello, honey. How's everything going?"

It wasn't her mother's normal solid, steady tone. Instead, her voice held notes of tension and fake cheerfulness. "Today was very productive. I met Sam and my... Audrey." Saying the word *grandmother* out loud didn't feel comfortable yet, and might never, but she held out hope. "They were both very nice, and I'm going over to their house for dinner on Thursday night." Silence greeted Alex from the other end of the phone line. "You can take a breath. They don't know who I am."

"How did you manage an invitation to dinner?"

Alex hung one leg off the side of the canvas to make the hammock rock. "I happened to be in the café that Sam owns, and she came in. She asked my landlord and his nephew over for dinner and I got included in the deal."

"I see."

"I know you warned me this would be hard, and you were right."

"For once, I'm not happy about being right."

"I know you're set on keeping this secret, but—"

"Alex, I just wanted to protect you...from what I

went through, but I realize that wasn't fair of me."
Her words were choked, as if forced through tears.

"Are you crying?"

"No," she said, but her breath shuddered. "Maybe
just a little."

"Is there something you're not telling me? What
exactly happened that summer?"

"You know how a smell or sound can trigger a
memory? Well, I can hear the Hill Country night
sounds over the phone line, and memories of my
time with your father flooded in without warning."

"I'm sorry. Should I go inside?"

"No, don't apologize and don't go in. They're
beautiful memories. Your father was the love of
my life, and I like remembering him."

She could picture her mom twirling an auburn
curl around her finger and knew she wanted to talk
about her lost love. "Tell me more about your summer in Oak Hollow with my father."

"We spent many nights star-gazing, and he'd tell
me about the constellations and nocturnal animals."

"There's an unusual sound I'm hearing that I
can't identify. I'm not sure if it's a bird or insect."

"He would have known exactly what it was.
Charlie was a real nature boy and craved adventure. That's why he worked so hard to earn a position on the archeological dig team and went on that
trip to Belize. He was going to meet me in New
York when he returned. We had it all planned. We
were going to travel and then figure out where to
settle down." Kate cleared her throat and sighed.

"And where to get married. He gave me the emerald ring the night before he flew off on his grand adventure. His parents, especially his mother, hated the idea of him living anywhere but Oak Hollow. They thought I was the reason he wanted to travel, and it was all my fault he was considering living anywhere other than his hometown."

"Don't you think he would've wanted to go off and see the world even if he'd never met you?"

"Absolutely. I guess it was just easier for them to blame me than him."

"So I get my sense of adventure from him?" She was happy to hear her mother's chuckle.

"That and so much more. You laugh like him. Tilt your head like him when you're deep in thought. And even though he loved adventure, he's where you get your fear of heights."

Alex shuddered. Living in a city of tall buildings had proven problematic over the years.

"I wish your father could've known about you. He would've been over-the-moon excited. I found out I was pregnant a few days after I got the news that…he was gone. I was heartbroken. Completely devastated. You were the only thing I had left of him, and I wanted you all to myself. In our own little bubble. I wanted to protect you. That's all I've ever wanted. And I guess I was protecting myself, as well."

"From what?" She'd always accepted her mother's word that the decisions she'd made were the best thing for both of them, but now that she'd met some of her family and seen the town, she wanted to dig deeper into the past.

"I've told you about your grandfather being a powerful attorney. The Hargrove family also had a lot of connections to people at the state capitol. I was nineteen, single and had no family other than your aunt Sari and uncle Leo. At the time, I was terribly afraid they would try to take you away from me. Then, as the years passed, I just didn't know how to right what I'd done."

The heartache she heard in her mother's voice made her own chest tighten. "You never have to worry about them taking me away from you. Twenty-five is a little old for a custody battle," she said, hoping it would lighten the mood.

"Oh, my girl, anyone in their right mind would fight for you."

Luke doesn't want to fight for me.

The teakettle whistled on her mother's end of the line, and Alex could picture her making evening tea in her gold-and-blue kimono, and then settling on her favorite chair with a romance novel. "You're my mother and you have to believe that about me."

"I'm so sorry I've put you in this position."

"I understand, but please consider that it might be time to tell the truth and reveal my identity."

"That's all I've been thinking about since our last call. It was wrong of me to ask you to deny family, and I won't try to stop you from moving forward with this. Just do me one favor. Get to know them a bit first and feel out the situation *before* you tell them."

A rush of relief washed over her. "I can do that. Are you sure you don't want to join me here?"

"I don't think that's a good idea. They'll probably be more accepting of the news if it's just you. They're going to blame me for this. Just know that I *will* come to you if you really need me. I'll always be there for you."

"Thanks, Mom. I just want the chance to get to know them, even if they never know who I am. I'll call you after the dinner at their house and let you know how everything goes."

"All right. I love you, honey."

"Love you, too. Night, Mom." She ended the call, carefully swung both legs over the side and shifted into a sitting position. Just as she glanced up, a large shadow loomed over her. Her heart leaped into her throat, and she jerked back hard enough to make the hammock flip and elicit the kind of girly scream she hated.

"It's just me. It's Walker."

With her pulse hammering, legs sticking straight up in the air and the back of her head resting in the grass, she put a hand to her racing heart. "You scared the crap out of me!" As she struggled to right herself, his large, warm hands clasped both of her ankles, slid slowly up her calves, past her knees, and eased her back into a sitting position.

She grasped his forearms for balance, loving the sensation of his muscles flexing as he gripped her thighs. Something—that was undeniably *not* fright—fluttered in her belly. With the light from the kitchen window shining behind him, he appeared larger than usual and was not giving off his normal frosty vibe.

"I didn't mean to frighten you. Sorry."

His fingers trailed away from her skin, and he tucked his hands under his biceps like he was forcing himself to keep them off her. When the moonlight lit his face, he didn't look the least bit sorry. In fact, he looked like he wanted to burst into laughter.

"I think you're one of those people who laughs when someone falls down," she said.

"And I think that high-pitched sound you made might've scared away all of the nightlife."

"Humph. Very funny. I can't figure you out, Officer Walker. I don't know if you just enjoy teasing me, or if you dislike me that much." She stood, ready to rush across the yard.

He caught her by the hand, but this time he didn't let go or pull away. "Alexandra..." He tucked a lock of hair behind her ear and his touch lingered on her cheek. "I like you."

Warmth flushed her skin, and she very much wanted him to kiss her. "You do?"

He moaned as if in pain and pulled her closer, his lips a breath away from her ear. "My life right now... It's..."

"Complicated?" she asked, finishing his sentence for him.

"Yeah." His embrace tightened, one arm circled

her waist while his other hand drifted up to massage the back of her neck and they swayed as if dancing to the music of the night. "I've made promises. I have new responsibilities. A child is depending on me."

"I understand. I really do." This man was dealing with a lot, and she was only here for a month. It wouldn't be fair to complicate his life for selfish moments of pleasure. But that didn't mean she wasn't disappointed. Alex rested her head on his chest to keep from giving in to temptation and kissing him.

He buried his fingers in her hair. "Maybe we can…"

For one brief moment she thought he'd suggest something more between them. Maybe a short-term fling. But his weary sigh said more than words. "We could stop irritating one another and agree to be friends?" she said, and then felt the vibration of a groan deep in his chest. Did friends dance like this? With no music but the shared beating of their hearts?

"Yes. Friends. That's best."

A disappointing answer, but the one she expected. Even though her fingers tingled with the need to touch his bare skin and have him do the same, she lifted her head, kissed his cheek and stepped out of his embrace, instantly missing the connection. "What's Cody doing?"

"He fell asleep as soon as his head hit the pillow. I was about to lock the back door but heard your voice."

Oh, no! What did he hear me saying?

"How long were you out here before you scared me?"

"Not long."

"I was talking to my mother."

"Yeah, I gathered that."

So he had heard some of her conversation. Her brain scrambled to remember what incriminating information he might've heard on her end of the call. "I should go take a shower."

A cold one.

"Good night." She practically ran for the back door.

Luke settled onto the hammock she'd vacated and listened to the whirr of cicadas in the trees. They were almost as loud as his screaming libido. He hadn't expected—and certainly hadn't planned—the physical contact with Alexandra, but after holding her in his arms, letting her sweet herbal scent fill his senses, he wanted a whole lot more than her friendship. He wanted to feel her skin burning against his. Feel her tremble and come alive in his arms. He shifted his jeans, which had become uncomfortably tight due to the state she'd put him in. If she hadn't suggested friendship—only seconds before he was about to kiss her—he probably would've made love to her all night long.

Maybe just once... No!

She was not the kind of woman he *needed* to find for himself and Cody. She would be leaving Oak Hollow and moving on with her life across the country. A long-distance romance would be no good for any of them.

He rubbed both hands over his face. What he should be concentrating on was overhearing her talk about a custody battle, telling the truth and revealing her identity. Who was the lovely, mysterious Alexandra Roth? Someone's secret love child? Because there was a family that she seemed very eager to know. And if he was on the right track, he didn't even want to think about which Hargrove male could possibly be her father.

He didn't believe she was up to anything nefarious. But he did believe she had information that might rock somebody's world, and he needed to find out what it was before he took her into the Hargrove home. Luke rolled and heaved himself up and out of the hammock. He needed to get to the truth of her reason for being here. Experience had taught him that pushing for information too hard and fast only led to someone shutting him out. The way he'd been keeping her on edge and at a distance was the wrong way to go about evidence gathering. It was time to cease irritating her to the point of frustration. Being friends with a woman he wanted in his bed could be good for him. Build his willpower. Be an exercise in restraint and control.

Am I really giving myself a pep talk about the positives of not having sex?

After locking up, he went to see if she'd talk to him some more, but his bedroom door was closed. He pressed his palm against the varnished wood. "Alexandra?"

Chapter Seven

Alex heard Luke outside the bedroom door and almost opened it when he said her name, but chickened out. There might be questions she didn't want to answer. Questions that could trip her up and make her reveal things she shouldn't. Things she needed to keep hidden for a little longer.

"Good night, Alexandra."

Goose bumps lifted across her skin in a warm satisfying wave. The way he used her full name, said in his deep, sexy Southern drawl, never failed to send tingles to her core. "Sweet dreams," she whispered, knowing he couldn't hear her reply, but wishing it for him all the same.

The lines of writing in her notebook blurred, and she rubbed her fatigued eyes. A good night's sleep would help her deal with whatever he threw her way tomorrow. When she reached to turn off the lamp, her pen rolled behind the bedside table. She climbed out of bed and pulled the furniture away from the wall. Along with her pen, she also found a dusty sheet of paper. She tucked it under his detective novel, and didn't mean to read it, but Cody's name caught her eye, and she couldn't resist.

Cody is my number one priority. Don't slip back into old ways. No fling is worth taking time away from him. No one-night stand is worth it. Don't do it. He comes first. Always think of Cody.

The note began and ended with the most important word—his nephew's name, and the reason he had changed his ways. She leaned her hip against the dresser and sighed. This was a note to remind himself of his priorities. And, apparently, a warning not to be the ladies' man he'd once been. She picked up his family photo and traced the line of his jaw. "Officer Luke Walker, you are a multilayered man. And you've got a lot on your plate."

She respected the sacrifices he was making for his nephew and would put aside her own desires. Suggesting friendship had been the correct move. Luke had to be placed firmly in the friends-only zone. That decision left her both proud of herself for considering their needs, and at the same time, yearning for the romance that might've been. After turning off the light, she settled in his sheets, his scent surrounding her, the echo of his touch lingering on her skin in every spot he'd caressed. Her cheek. That sensitive place on her neck that made her tremble. The dip at the small of her back.

The deep, longing ache for his hands and lips on her body followed her into lovely dreams.

Alex woke to the sounds of Cody and Luke getting ready for the day. She rolled out of bed, went through her morning routine and then made her way to the kitchen for a cup of liquid wake-me-up. Luke wasn't shirtless like the day before, but he was still enticing in his blue uniform, a thumb hooked on his wide utility belt.

A sleepy-eyed little boy sat at the kitchen table swirling the last bits of colorful cereal around his bowl.

"Good morning, boys."

"Morning." Luke downed the last of his coffee and put his mug into the sink. "We should be home around six tonight. I wrote my cell number on that pad just in case you need to call me. Of course, you can call the police station, as well. They can always get ahold of me."

She made her way to the coffeepot and poured a cup. "Well…when I get myself into trouble, they'll probably just bring me down to the station."

"I'll make sure to get a jail cell ready for you," he said, a playful grin transforming his face.

"Uncle Luke, you can't put her in jail."

"I'm just teasing. I wouldn't really put her in handcuffs," he said and then winked at Alex over the top of the child's head.

She almost spit a mouthful of coffee onto the floor. Maybe she was still asleep and dreaming.

He glanced at his watch. "Cody, get your boots on, please. I need to drop you off and get to work."

"No. Stay and plant flowers," he said.

"Sorry, buddy. I have to work today."

"No work!" the little boy yelled and banged his spoon against the table.

"Hey, no yelling," Luke said.

Cody shoved his chair backward, crawled under the kitchen table and wrapped both arms around his knees.

Luke's jaw tightened, and he glanced at the ceiling as if searching for strength and patience.

Alex sat cross-legged on the floor facing the angry child. "I won't plant any flowers without you. I promise. When you get home tonight, we can get started on planting. How does that sound?"

Cody flicked his gaze her way then lay on his back and kicked the underside of the table.

Milk sloshed onto the yellow surface, and Luke grabbed the bowl and put it into the sink.

"You can spend the day playing with Hannah." She continued speaking to him in a soothing voice and ignored the bad behavior. "This evening, we can work in the yard and then play some songs on my guitar. Oh, and try out the keyboard. But right now, it's time to get started on your day. You don't want to make your uncle late for work."

His banging stopped. "Play music tonight?"

"Yes, after we all do what we need to during the day. Time to get going, little man. Spit spot." She clapped her hands, hoping the *Mary Poppins* saying would get him moving.

Cody crawled out from under the table, grabbed his boots from a rack by the back door and walked into the living room.

"Thank you," Luke called after him and then turned to face Alex. "Thanks for the help. That was impressive. It usually takes a lot longer to redirect him when he gets like that."

"No problem. I'm glad I could help." She grinned up at him from her spot on the floor, hoping it was contagious and that she could lighten his distraught mood. "Have a good day at work, Officer."

He reached out a hand and pulled her to her feet, the crease between his eyebrows softening as he returned her smile. "You, too."

His fingers brushing against her palm made her insides tingle. If he continued to touch her and smile like that, this *friendship* thing was going to be a challenge. Who was she kidding? It was a massive test of willpower. She followed them onto the front porch and waved as they drove away, then she sat on the swing and finished her coffee while birds sang and neighbors walked their dogs.

On her way to the cemetery an hour later, she took note of interesting landscaping she'd like to recreate in Luke's yard, but thinking that way was a dangerous dream. She reached into the pocket of her denim shorts and rubbed the polished piece of quartz she'd brought with her from New York. If she was lucky, placing a stone on her father's grave would give her a sense of peace and a bit of the connection she longed for.

Stories about him were limited to the short time her parents had been together, and she was eager to see if she could get her grandparents and uncle to talk about him. But she had to admit that her mother was smart to suggest getting to know her father's family and feeling out the situation before the big reveal.

Even with her initial warm welcome, would Audrey Hargrove change her tune once she learned the secret that had been withheld from her for so many years? Would blame toward her mother transfer to her? She'd be in Texas for a month and had time to get to know them. She'd go to their house for dinner and see if his childhood photos were displayed. That might be a good starter for asking questions, and then she'd take it one step at a time after that.

A gust of wind rustled the limbs above, and dappled light filtered through the trees, creating ever-changing patterns on the concrete surface. Alex brushed unruly hair from her eyes and quickened her steps, her mind feeling much the same as the moving shadows. A block down Cypress Creek, the arched metal sign for the Oak Hollow cemetery came into view. She entered through an old ironwork gate that creaked and groaned when she pushed it open. Old marble stones filled the back corner. Newer, modern ones were spread in front of her and to the right.

Alex started on one side of the newer section and walked up and down several rows before finding an area with the name *Hargrove* scribed on several stones, but there was no sign of a grave for Charles Alexander Hargrove. Disappointment settled heavy in her chest. She methodically searched the entire cemetery two times with no luck. Could it be that his body had never been recovered? Was there a memorial somewhere but no grave? Was there a second cemetery? Once again, she studied each Hargrove marker, but none of the dates could possibly be her father.

Discouraged, sad and hot, she sat down in the shade of a large oak tree near Cody's mother's grave. "Your brother and son sure do miss you. And I can tell you were a fantastic mother. Luke is very devoted to Cody, and I think they will be just fine." After sitting and enjoying the shade for several minutes, she put the stone she'd brought on Libby's pink granite marker and left the cemetery.

She pulled out her phone to search for information about her father's grave, but she didn't have any internet connection. Maybe it was better this way. She had always preferred to learn things firsthand rather than tracking down dry facts on some website. She'd waited twenty-five years and could wait to see what was revealed at the Hargrove family dinner.

Hargrove family dinner.

Those were words she'd never thought to say. On her return walk to Luke's house, she considered calling her mother and telling her she hadn't found his grave, but there was no reason to upset her until she had more information.

She spent the rest of the morning working on the song she'd started and a watercolor painting of Luke and Cody strolling down the sidewalk.

That afternoon, Alex sat on the front porch swing sketching some more detailed landscape ideas for Luke's backyard. She chuckled to herself just imagining his reaction to some of her more outlandish ideas. No doubt, he would not approve of many of them.

A maroon SUV pulled up and parked in front of the house. Tess, Hannah and Cody climbed out, and the children ran up the front walk.

"Hey, kids. What are you up to?"

"We plant flowers," Hannah said, then twirled and fell onto her bottom in the grass.

Cody stood behind her and pulled her to her feet. For a little boy who shied away from touch, he didn't hesitate to help his friend. His compassion and kindness melted Alex's heart.

Tess followed the children onto the porch. "Good afternoon. I hope we aren't interrupting anything?"

"Not at all. I'm glad for the company."

"Cody insisted we come over and see about helping you with the plants you bought yesterday."

"Excellent." She closed her sketchbook and rose

from the swing. "Cody, do you know if your uncle has any garden tools?"

He nodded and motioned for them to follow and then led them around to the detached garage. They gathered the tools they needed and loaded them into a red wheelbarrow. They started their work in the front of the house and then moved into the back-yard with the last trays of flowers. Having the children's help truthfully made more work, but Alex didn't mind one bit.

She stacked empty plastic pots and put them into the wheelbarrow. "Tess, is there more than one cemetery in town?"

"No. Just the one."

"Momma! Worm. Ewww." Hannah giggled and bounced from foot to foot.

"It won't hurt you," Tess said.

Cody picked it up, and as if to prove the point, he draped it across his bare arm and held it close to the little girl's face.

She squealed and ran around in circles.

Alex chuckled at the mischievous grin on Cody's face, thinking it rather matched his uncle's.

When they'd planted the last pot of daisies, Alex sat on the steps of the back deck and took a big gulp of water. "I'm sweaty."

"I so wetty, too." Hannah wiped a dirt-covered hand across her forehead and flung her head back dramatically. "So-o-o wetty."

Cody giggled at Hannah's misunderstanding of the word and the adults joined in.

"I have an idea," Alex said. "Since we're done with our work, let's turn on that sprinkler and run through it to cool off."

Cody stopped laughing and shook his head. "No shower."

Alex moved from her spot and kneeled before him in the grass. "It's okay. It's not like a shower, but you don't have to do it if you don't want to. I'll get you one of the juice Popsicles I saw in the freezer, and you can sit on the deck."

He nodded and took a seat in one of the Adirondack chairs while she got a treat for both kids.

Tess helped Alex unwind the garden hose, and they attached the type of sprinkler that would slowly sweep its fan of water back and forth across the grass.

Still in their clothes, the three girls ran through the spray of water with Hannah in the middle holding their hands.

Cody watched intently, but he didn't move from his spot in the chair.

After a few minutes, Alex went over to check on him. She was dripping wet and tucked a loose strand of hair behind her ear. "The water feels really good, and I'm not so hot and sticky anymore. Are you sure you don't want to try it?"

He looked back and forth between her and then Tess and Hannah playing in the water, but didn't respond.

"What if we just stand at the edge and you can

decide if you want to go in or not? I promise I won't make you touch the water if you don't want to."

He finally stood and followed her into the yard. The fan of water from the sprinkler came their way, and Alex reached out to let the droplets land on her hands. When the water swung back in the other direction, he held out one hand. When the cool water splattered on his fingers, he gasped but then smiled.

"It's nice and cool, isn't it?" she asked him.

Each time the arc of water came their way, he scooted a half step closer until his whole arm got wet.

"That's great, Cody. You are doing so good," Alex said.

"Come, Cody," Hannah cheered and bounced on her toes. "You can do it."

"If you want, we can run through the edge of the water together. Want to try it?" Alex asked.

"Come play." Hannah danced right across the center of the sprinkler.

The little boy looked up with uncertainty crossing his face before he took a deep breath and nodded.

"Want to hold my hand?"

He reached tentatively forward but then pulled away. After mumbling something to himself, he finally put his hand into her open palm.

As promised, she only ran through the very edge of the spray, with him on the outside. "How was that?"

Cody wiped his face. "I'm okay."

His shocked expression made her smile. "You are so brave. Want to try it again?"

"Okay. I'm okay."

He held on to her a little tighter as she ran closer to the center of the water. His little hand clung to hers and his happy, childish giggle sent a bolt of maternal longing straight to her heart, and her womb.

This was the kind of life she wanted. A house with a yard. A child. A family. She couldn't wait to be a mother. If for some reason having her own children never worked out, she would most definitely consider adoption. There were bound to be tons of kids like Cody who didn't have a loving uncle to take them in.

Luke spotted Tess's car as he pulled around to the back and stopped in front of the garage. When he closed the truck door, laughter and squeals came from the backyard. That made him smile, but the sound of Cody's high-pitched scream sent fear streaking through him, and his heart dropped. He ran, flung open the back gate and couldn't believe what he was seeing. Alex had his nephew by the hand, and she was pulling him through the spraying water.

Luke's anger spiked. "Alexandra! What the hell are you doing? I told you he's afraid of water."

Their laughter stopped, and the four of them turned to him with open mouths.

How could she traumatize Cody like this? Tess should have known better than to allow this to happen. He crossed the yard with quick strides and pulled Cody into his arms, but his nephew was no longer screaming and didn't even look upset. He was smiling.

"Are you okay, buddy?"

He nodded. "I'm wet."

"I can see that." He could also see both women glaring at him and Hannah clinging to her mother's leg.

"It's fun," Cody added. "Do it, Uncle Luke."

"You want me to run through the water?" He couldn't believe what he was hearing. He looked down at his uniform, but if Cody wanted to go into a shower of water, he'd do it no matter what he was wearing. "Are you sure?"

"Yes. Do it. Do it. Do it."

Something loosened inside his chest as he put the boy on his feet. Luke did as he was asked, and even though Cody held his hand with the strength of a vise grip, his nephew giggled the whole time. The sound lightened the worry weighing on his heart and he felt on the verge of very unmanly tears.

"Again, Uncle Luke."

"I'd love to." After one more pass across the yard, he wiped water from his eyes. "Can you give me a minute to go inside and take off my uniform?" After a nod of approval, he gave Cody a hug and rushed inside, still avoiding the glares of two women.

The first thing he noticed was the kitchen table half covered with watercolor supplies. One of Cody caught his eye. She'd captured his nephew's likeness with startling accuracy. His frustration with her messiness eased, until he stepped into the dining room and caught sight of that table in a similar state with sheets of music and balled-up paper. He shook his head and sighed. He didn't want to waste time cleaning it up right now. It could wait, and hopefully Cody wouldn't be upset by it when he came inside.

He locked his service weapon in the safe and changed his clothes as quickly as he could. He didn't want to miss a second more of his nephew's breakthrough. An uncomfortable flicker of jealousy stirred within. He was envious of Alexandra's ability to get his nephew to smile and try new things. He wanted to be the one to put those joyous expressions on Cody's sad little face. He wanted to be able to calm his tantrums and get him past his fears.

He rejoined them dressed in a pair of swim trunks, but before he could return to the water play, Tess met him at the kitchen door and smacked him upside the back of his head.

"That's for jumping to conclusions and yelling at Alex. You know I'd never let anything bad happen to Cody."

He blew out a slow breath. "I know. It was a gut reaction to hearing him scream. I might have overreacted."

"You think?" Tess moved forward like she might strike again.

Both children ran up onto the deck and saved

him from further abuse. With a kid holding each of his hands, they pulled him along into the yard.

He forced himself to make eye contact with Alexandra, expecting her to glare at him again, but she smiled, her eyes alight with merriment. Who was this woman? And why did she have to look so tempting with droplets of water glistening on her long legs, bared by denim shorts, and a wet, pale blue T-shirt molding to her generous curves? Thankfully, she had on a bra, but that didn't keep his blood from thudding hot in his veins.

He rubbed a hand over his face, forcefully blocking out the tempting view. He couldn't forget that he had to get her talking about why she'd really come to Oak Hollow. And he had to do it before taking her to the Hargroves' home. Yelling at her had not been the best start to that goal.

"Hannah Lynn," Tess called to her daughter and held out a towel. "Come dry off. We need to get home."

"No go, Momma."

"Your daddy and Nan are waiting to eat dinner with us."

That got the little girl's attention, and she ran to her mother. After goodbyes, Hannah and Tess left, and it was suddenly much quieter in the backyard.

Cody grabbed Luke's hand and then held his free hand out to Alex. "One more time."

There was no way either of them was going to tell him no. He'd made big strides in overcoming a fear and it was time to celebrate, even if the yard turned into a swamp. The three of them ran back and forth through the soggy grass, mud squishing between their toes.

"I'm starving," Luke said. "Who wants pizza?"

"Me, me, me." Cody sang the words then repeated them again in a deeper tone as if he was trying out different voices.

"I'll call in the order." Luke rubbed his hair, flinging water droplets. "Are you okay with pepperoni? That's the only kind Cody will eat."

"Works for me." Alexandra turned off the water and unscrewed the sprinkler.

"Cody, let's get your bath before the food arrives."

"But…" The little boy looked at his uncle like he was crazy. "I'm already wet."

"You're also splattered with mud and grass."

"Come over here," she called to them. "Let me rinse off everyone's feet before we go inside."

Cody came willingly but insisted the hose only ran at a trickle so there was no danger of a sudden splash. Once he was semiclean, he ran ahead of them toward the back door.

"Alexandra, while I get him cleaned up, could you clear off the tables?"

She clasped a hand to her mouth. "I'm so sorry. I meant to have the house all neat and tidy before you two got home this evening. When Tess and the kids arrived, we got busy and I forgot all about my stuff still being out. I'll do it now."

Before he could add that he was sorry for yelling at her, she rushed into the house.

Food was ordered and one little boy was finally talked into a bath, because even though he'd played in the sprinkler, he still wouldn't entertain the idea of a shower. The three of them sat down at the kitchen table for a supper of delivery pizza and the fruit Alexandra insisted on adding to the meal.

"Is there music at the Fourth of July picnic?" she asked.

"There will be bands playing all day. I have to help build the stage on the square."

Cody's head snapped up and he looked almost directly at Alex. "More music?"

Luke paused in midbite, still surprised by the way his nephew talked directly to her. It usually took him weeks or even months to warm up to someone new.

"Of course. I promised." Alexandra added an apple slice to the little boy's plate. "We'll play music after we finish eating. And then we should go outside to see the moon. It's supposed to be a clear night, and we should have a good view of the night sky."

She was making it mighty tough not to kiss her, especially when she smiled at his nephew like she truly adored him. Why did she have to be so darn tempting with her damp hair curling around her cheeks and all traces of makeup washed away? She always looked beautiful, but he particularly liked it when she was completely natural with nothing artificial to hide her beauty. And he couldn't help but lean in every once in a while to inhale the scent of her bodywash. Something fruity and fresh that made him want to slide his tongue along every inch of her skin until—

"Uncle Lu-u-uke." Cody waved a hand in his face. "Are you listening?"

"Sorry, buddy. What did you say?" This woman had him woolgathering and planning things he'd like to do with her in private. Things he shouldn't be thinking about at the dinner table, or anywhere for that matter. He should be focused on Cody.

After the kitchen was tidied up, the old keyboard was dusted off and plugged in, the guitar was tuned and, at Cody's request, he and Alexandra alternated between the two instruments.

"Do you want to try playing that chord?" she asked her eager student.

When he nodded and held out his arms for the guitar, she positioned it on his lap and reached around his small shoulders to place her hands over his. "Put your fingers right here. Now, hold the pick with the other hand and move it across the strings."

Cody strummed, and his golden-brown eyes lit up when the note rang from the instrument. "I did it."

"Way to go, buddy," Luke said from his spot across the room, where he pretended to work on his laptop. "That sounds amazing."

The other amazing thing was the way his nephew allowed Alexandra to touch him so frequently and to this extent. Although he was very happy to see joy on his nephew's face, jealousy reared its unwelcome head once again. He tried not to let it bother him that it was Alexandra, and not him, who'd helped his nephew make a breakthrough on getting past his anxiety about water. But it did bother him. He wanted to be the one to help him past fears, make him smile, get him talking and ease his sadness. He was being ridiculous, but feelings were feelings, and he couldn't stop the ones filling his head. Luke left the room and went to the kitchen for a beer.

As soon as Cody fell asleep, it would be time for a serious talk with this curious woman. Intuition, plus overhearing her phone call, told him there was more to her long visit than simple relaxation, and he had to discover her true reason for coming across the country to Oak Hollow. He would not be responsible for taking her into William and Audrey Hargrove's home without knowing what potential trouble she might cause.

Chapter Eight

Alex sat on a deck chair under the starry sky, the soothing sights and sounds of nature easing some of her worries. After looking at the moon, then insisting she sing him to sleep like Mary Poppins, Cody had finally drifted into dreamland, and his uncle had run off to the shower like he couldn't get away from her fast enough. He'd watched their music session, and at first appeared happy and proud of his nephew, but his mood had shifted to something darker. Had she done something wrong? Again? Knowing where she stood with Luke Walker was always a bit of a mystery.

She hung her long hair over the back of the Adirondack chair and tried not to picture him wet and naked in the shower. But trying did no good in this case. Her vivid artist's imagination filled in the blanks with amazing details. Iridescent soap bubbles languidly sliding over hard dips and planes on their journey down to those sexy muscles that angled inward beside his hip bones. The ones that seemed to point to that "happy trail" of dark hair she'd glimpsed above his running shorts. One she'd like to travel with her hands. And tongue. An inner warmth flushed her skin. If she couldn't have him in real life, a fantasy affair would have to do. No one could take that away.

The back door opened, and the man on her mind slipped into the chair beside hers. He put a beer to his mouth and took a long pull, as if it was filled with liquid courage.

How silly was she to be envious of the amber bottle touching his lips? "I'm sorry if I overstepped with Cody."

He handed her a second cold bottle and raised his eyes to meet hers. "I'm the one who should be apologizing for yelling at you. I'm really sorry about that."

"At first, I wanted to kick your cowboy butt, but I thought about it and realized how the scene must've looked when you came into the backyard. You were only trying to protect him. I get it." She took a sip of the beer he'd given her, fully expecting to hate it. The rim was salty, and a hint of lime hit her taste buds. It was actually pretty good, and she took another drink. "Are you really okay with me teaching him to play guitar and piano?"

"Of course. He loves it. I'll have to find him some lessons after you leave."

"You definitely should. He has a lot of natural talent and ability. Did he get it from you?"

"Nope. Not me or my sister."

A breeze gusted across her skin, bringing the scent of magnolia blossoms. "What happened to Cody's father?"

"He never had one."

"Me, neither." *Oh, snap. Why'd I bring up fathers?* She stared straight ahead but could feel him studying her profile.

"My sister, Libby, was thirteen years older and became a mother to me after our parents died. I was nine, and she put her life on hold for me. When she hit her midthirties, and didn't see marriage in her future, she decided to use a sperm donor. She really wanted to have a baby, and she went for it. She was always good at going after what she wanted."

"Good for her. So you know a bit about what your nephew is going through?"

"I do," he said, and picked at the label on his bottle. "Sometimes I feel responsible for her giving up too much of her own life for her annoying little brother."

"I bet she was happy to do it. And I think you are repaying any debts owed." From the corner of her eye, she watched his long fingers brush through his wet hair, making the short strands stand up in spikes.

"I try my best. You're an only child?"

"Yes."

"You said once that it's always been just you and your mother."

"That's right. I also have a great aunt and uncle who live close." Uncomfortable with the direction of the conversation, she set her bottle on the deck and wrapped her arms around her middle.

"Have you ever met your father?"

Her thudding pulse skyrocketed. He knew something. She could feel it. "No."

"And you've come to find him?"

Direct hit. His question struck like a bee sting. Unable to sit still a second longer, she jumped to her feet and paced across the deck. Given her inability to convincingly fib combined with his detective skills, she shouldn't have been surprised at this outcome.

"Please tell me it's not old man Hargrove. That would kill his wife, Audrey."

"No!" Her throat went dry. "It's definitely not him." A sheen of sweat formed on her face and she fanned her warm cheeks.

"But it *is* someone in the Hargrove family?" He stood and stepped into her path, catching her by the shoulders right before she crashed into him. "Whoa, Alexandra, you're trembling."

Her insides quivered, and she blew out a long, slow breath. There was no way to hide a bomb that had already detonated. "It's Charles Hargrove. Please don't say anything. Not yet." The front of his shirt was fisted in her hands and a tear trickled down her cheek. "I promised my mom I'd get to know them and feel out the situation before telling anyone who I am. I swear I'm not here to cause any harm or ask for anything."

Luke wrapped his arms around her, cradling her against his body. "Calm down. Take a breath." He stroked her hair and murmured soothing sounds in her ear.

The balanced rhythm of his heart beating against her cheek helped to steady her own rapid pounding. "I just want to know something about where I come from. I'm not here to wreck anyone's life," she said into the soft fabric of his shirt.

"I won't say anything. Not until you're ready."

She lifted her head and their gazes locked. His expression was concerned, but open and understanding. "Really? You'll keep my secret until the time is right?"

"Yes, I will."

Without pausing to consider what she was doing, she pressed her lips to his for a quick, chaste kiss. "Thank you so much. I…" Her breath froze when his warm hand cupped her cheek.

"Just promise you'll keep me in the loop and talk to me about what's happening. I don't want anyone getting hurt, and I don't like seeing you cry." He stroked the corner of her mouth with his thumb, making her lips part on a soft, shuddering exhale.

"Luke…" One intimate touch and she was lost to the startling depth of the sensation. She clung to his lean waist, curling her fingers around the taut muscles running along his spine. If she raised on her toes just the slightest bit their lips would touch, and she could sate the desire reflected in his dark, moody eyes.

While struggling to remind herself of his unique situation and all the reasons she should step away, he closed the distance, and there was nothing chaste about his kiss. Full lips teasing, sucking gently, and teeth softly nipping. She eagerly opened and let the pleasure course through her blood. Slow, heady exploration left her dizzy and thankful for the support of his arms securely fitting her body against his.

"Alexandra," he whispered against her mouth. "I don't know how to do this friendship thing with you. Especially with you sleeping under my roof."

"Me, neither, but I'll be moving to the hotel right after the holiday weekend."

"I'm not sure how much that will help," he responded in a voice that had grown huskier.

"What if we limit ourselves to only kissing?" With her fingers sliding into his hair, she traced her tongue along the seam of his lips, eliciting a hungry growl that made her ache for so much more. In a perfect situation they'd have no reason not to be the single adults they were. No reason to resist sharing their pleasure. But this was not the perfect situation. "So what do you think about upgrading our friendship to a friends-with-*only*-kissing-benefits package?"

"Kissing-benefits package?" His eyebrows winged

up and a broad grin made his eyes crinkle at the corners.

Suddenly feeling ridiculous, she ducked her head. "It's just an idea, but I guess it's juvenile and stupid. I sound like I'm in junior high."

His hands dipped lower on her hips, long fingers splayed. "There's nothing stupid about it. But I do have one question." His mouth teased a very sensitive spot behind her ear. "Do I have to keep it above the neck?" Before she could form a reply, he trailed a searing line down to her shoulder and chuckled when she moaned and tilted her head to give him better access.

"Being a peace officer, you'll probably want to set some... Oh, that feels so good," she said on a sigh, and shivered as he sucked gently at the curve where her neck met her shoulder. "Rules. You'll probably want us to set some rules."

"Do you like rules, Alexandra?" His teeth closed gently on her earlobe.

She gasped and arched against him, feeling the full effect of what their physical contact was doing to him. "I like to follow some of them. Others, I enjoy breaking. I'm breaking a self-imposed rule right now."

"Which one is that?"

"This." She slid her hands up his back to curl around his shoulders and kissed the curve of his jaw. "And this." His chest was warm where her lips pressed the skin exposed by the V of his T-shirt.

Luke shivered under her exploration and squeezed

her hips. "I thought kissing was on the table for consideration?"

"Was it wrong of me to suggest such a thing?"

"Not when it's something we both want."

"Just last night I told myself I would stick to only being your friend, and *nothing* more. I should really work on my willpower." She dropped her forehead to his chest and breathed in his woodsy cedar scent. "I don't want to do anything that will be bad for you or Cody. I know he must come first for you. As he should."

"I appreciate that. And while that's true, I don't think kissing you will jeopardize my nephew in any way. Not if we are private and careful about our... physical contact." His fingers traveled up her sides, thumbs stroking, coming close to the swell of her breasts. "Show me what you want, Alexandra. Tell me what you need."

The dangerous request sizzled in her blood. What she wanted was a fantasy romance. "I need your mouth on mine." His lips were warm and welcoming, yielding under her deep, exploring kiss. Stark pleasure streaked through her blood, proving the expression "weak in the knees" was not just a clichéd myth.

A light flicked on at the house next door.

"Luke," she whispered and kissed him once more. "Can your neighbors see us?"

"It's possible with my porch light on. Let's go chill out on the hammock."

"Good idea. There's only so much you can do in that thing without getting flipped into the grass."

"Wanna bet?" Luke kept an arm around her waist and led her across the yard. After lying down first, he stretched out his arm and motioned for her to take the spot beside him.

"Are you sure? I might send us tumbling."

"I'll risk it."

She eased down beside him and rested her head on his bicep. Only a few days ago, she'd thought he was a complete male-chauvinist jerk, but she'd been wrong. Luke was starting to reveal parts of himself that she'd caught hints of. Parts she suspected he only showed to those closest to him. His understanding nature had soothed her anxiety so quickly after having her secret discovered.

"I love that tree." She pointed to the large oak that resembled her tattoo. "It looks like the kind fairies might live in." An animal she couldn't identify started a whirring noise. "What is that sound?"

"Fairies." He chuckled when her mouth dropped open. "It's cicadas. Listen and wait for what happens next." The call was quickly answered by hundreds more. The sound grew and built to a frenzied pitch that spread across the treetops to encompass the night.

"I've never heard anything like that in the city. And what about that deep sound that we hear every now and then? That one. Hear it?"

"That's a bullfrog. There's a creek in the greenbelt behind the yard."

"This is the kind of night that songs are written about."

He trailed his fingers up and down her arm. "What kind of song would you write about me? A sad country song?"

"Hmmm." She tapped a finger against her chin. "I'm not sure yet. Tell me more about yourself."

"What you see is pretty much what you get."

"I don't believe that for a second." She was getting a look at his depth of character. The man she'd glimpsed a few times really was in there, hidden under aggravating comments and exasperating behavior. "I bet you and your sister had fun growing up in this town."

"It was pretty cool. I stayed out of trouble, mostly. I did a lot of fishing in the river, skateboarding and played sports."

"I heard about you being a star football player." *And a player when it comes to women.* That was another reason to keep this thing between them to a controlled level. Her curiosity took hold, and she couldn't resist a few probing questions. "Were you the kind of guy who dated the same girl through most of high school or lots of different girls? Maybe the head cheerleader?"

"I did date a cheerleader for part of my senior year. Tanya Martin. She was even the homecoming queen. We ended things before she left for college, and she never returned."

"And since high school, have you had many serious relationships?" She rubbed her bare foot against his and hoped she wasn't overstepping with her questions.

"A couple of years ago I had a girlfriend that I thought might lead to something, but it definitely didn't. Guess I'm not the serious-relationship kind of guy. Just casual dating."

From what she'd heard, *a lot* of casual dating. Good thing she wasn't staying in Oak Hollow and looking for a serious relationship with this Casanova cowboy. "I dated a guy that asked me to marry him after six months."

"And you thought it was too soon?"

"That wasn't why I said no. I think if it's meant to be, a couple can know in a very short amount of time, but it wasn't right with him. I didn't love Thomas, and he didn't love me. He just wanted me to be arm candy and host his parties." She'd never forget the embarrassment of Thomas calling her irresponsible in front of his friends and business partners. How was she to know they'd plow through the case of wine she'd bought for his gathering in an hour flat?

"You don't like planning parties?" He lifted her hand and pressed their palms together like he was measuring the length of her fingers.

"Not the kind of stuffy events he wanted. Your birthday was the fun kind of gathering. I've been wondering something. Why didn't you want to have a party?"

"No one knows what a big deal my sister always made of my birthday, and it was my first one without her. When I was a kid, she always put a present on the foot of my bed so it would be the first thing I saw when I woke up. And she always made my favorite Italian cream cake with lots of pecans in the icing."

"The one at your party was chocolate. You didn't tell anyone your favorite kind of cake?"

"No. I have Libby's recipe box, but I didn't want to ask anyone to make it."

"I'll make it for you." She bit her lip, worried she'd gone too far with that offer, but he continued to stroke her arm and then rested his cheek on the top of her head. "Tell me something else about growing up in Oak Hollow."

"I worked at the hotel when I was a teenager. My sister managed the place, and we lived there after my parents died."

"Did you live in the suite with the kitchen that you said you'd get for me?"

"That's the one."

"And you don't think this 'being friends with partial benefits' will be easier once I move to the hotel?"

"No. Just less opportunity for moments like this." He tipped her face, shot her a mischievous smile and then sucked her lower lip before kissing her softly.

She barely restrained herself from slipping a hand under the hem of his T-shirt and playing her fingers along his six-pack abs like an instrument. "Rule number one really should be no kissing below the neck because that has way too much potential to lead to…more."

"Really?" He chuckled. "You're serious about the rules thing? Not sure I like it, but it's probably a wise idea. Is that the only rule?"

"No. If there's a one, there must be a two. So number two is… Hmmm. Let's see."

"Is it a big one?" He cupped the back of her knee and hiked her leg up and across his thighs.

Her train of thought derailed. Completely. All she could think about was his deep voice saying "a big one." If she moved her leg up, she might be able to discover just how big of a one she was dealing with. "I have no idea what rule number two should be."

"Well, since you're only here for a little while, we could agree that this is a short-term arrangement until you go home to New York?"

"That's a good one. I agree."

The sound of a crying baby in a nearby house carried through the night. Luke flinched and slid his hand from hers. The infant's cry was like an alarm blaring a warning about Luke's responsibility for the child inside his home, and it burst their sensual bubble. Cody was counting on him to get things right and be a good parent, and Luke was still struggling to find his footing. She had to remember that.

He slipped his arm out from under her. "I better go inside and check on Cody. I'm not sure if I'd hear him out here if he calls for me."

They untangled, and she let him pull her safely from the hammock. Without touching or teasing or any more discussion about rules, they went inside, through the kitchen and then dining room and down the short hallway.

"Good night, Alexandra." With his hands held firmly against his sides, he gave her one more quick peck on the lips at the door of his bedroom and then turned and walked away.

"Sweet dreams." Alex licked her lips, tasting his kiss and knowing that what he'd said was true. Agreeing to a set amount of time was the best and safest way to play out this sexual tension between them.

Now, all she had to do was follow the rules.
Stupid rules. What was I thinking?

Luke stretched out on his bed of sleeping bags and listened to his nephew's soft snoring, but he couldn't rest, not while flooded with visions of the intriguing beauty down the hall. The sensation of her coming alive in his arms had been intoxicating. She'd bewitched him and made him talk about things he held close and private. Made him do exactly what he knew was dangerous, and start something between them. Once he started going down this road with Alexandra, he feared he'd want... everything.

What spell had this wandering woman cast?

She'd mentioned breaking promises to herself and had been right about needing rules, because he was breaking vows of his own. When she'd first arrived and ignited attraction, he'd tried not to like her, but she made that impossible, especially when she did things like graciously accept his apology for yelling at her. Alexandra might be a bit quirky, but she was also very understanding, and so good with Cody. And she made him want her so badly he ached in more ways than one, but he'd do the friends-with-only-kissing-benefits thing and hope the practice would improve his self-control.

He slept fitfully and almost went to join her in his bedroom every time he woke in the night, but resisted the temptation. His nephew sleeping near him was a good reminder of where his priorities lay. Instead of sating his urges with things they'd agreed were against the rules, he suffered through a lonely night on the hard floor of a child's bedroom.

The next morning, the savory scents of home cooking—that were not his usual toast and cold cereal—woke him. He heaved himself off the sleeping bag, got ready for the day and took a moment to hover in the kitchen doorway and admire Alexandra in her tank top and tie-dyed pajama pants. She hummed and swayed her hips on her way from the refrigerator to the stove, her movements flowing like a graceful dance. His body took note, and he imagined that she moved in that same erotic dance in bed.

As if she'd heard his thoughts, she turned and

gave him a brilliant smile. "Good morning. Are you hungry?"

Hungry for you.

"Always." He crossed the room intending to give her a by-the-rules, above-the-neck morning kiss, but Cody popped out from the pantry, and Luke stopped himself right before pulling her into his arms.

"Brown sugar," the little boy yelled at top volume and handed the bag to Alex.

"Thank you. Let's sprinkle some of this on the oatmeal and we can eat."

He and Cody always sat at the table for meals, but something about the addition of a third person made it feel different. Like a real family breakfast. It was probably just the plate of sausages, the pile of biscuits and the bowls of steaming oatmeal. Or maybe it was because it was Alexandra sitting across from him, talking about the dream she'd had and her plans for the day, and looking gorgeous with her long hair piled into a messy bun. The woman was captivating both him and his nephew.

He shoved the thought of her becoming part of their family out of his mind, because it was out of the question. Her home was far away, and she had a life she'd be going back to.

After breakfast, Luke put his empty dishes into the sink beside the heaping stack she'd created while cooking. It was something he'd quickly grown to expect. "Cody, time to get dressed. We need to leave in about fifteen minutes."

Cody crossed his arms over his chest and stood beside Alex. "I'm staying with *my* Mary Poppins."

Luke mimicked his nephew's stance, but the corner of his mouth trembled with the threat of a smile. "How is it you figure she's *your* Mary Poppins?"

"'Cause I asked Mommy to send her from the sky."

The statement struck him square in the heart like a searing blade. He turned away and pressed his knuckles against his mouth, unwilling to allow the flash of emotion to escape in front of anyone. He'd sent up the same kind of prayers and wishes after his parents died and knew all too well the pain this little boy was feeling.

Alexandra rubbed circles on his back. "He can stay with me. I promise I'll take good care of him."

A deep breath in. A slow release. And he found his voice. "You don't mind? I don't want to mess with your plans."

"My plans are totally flexible. I'd love to spend the day with Cody."

He kneeled before his nephew. "Will you promise to be a very good boy for Alexandra?"

"Yes. I'm a good boy."

"You sure are. I love you, buddy. Have fun today." He ruffled his nephew's hair and wiped his eye before a tear fell.

She followed him outside onto the porch. "Is it okay if we walk to the square and check out some of the shops?"

"That's fine."

"I'd like to look for a kite."

He reached for her hand and laced their fingers together, craving the comfort of her touch. "Mackintosh's Five and Dime probably has kites. Call me if you're in town around lunch and maybe I can meet y'all at the Acorn Café."

"That sounds perfect. Have a good morning at work, Officer Walker."

He pulled their joined hands to his lips and kissed her knuckles. "You, too, Miss Poppins."

On the short drive to work, he connected to Bluetooth and called Tess.

"Morning, Walker. Are you running late?" she asked.

"No, but Cody won't be coming over today. He wanted to stay with Alexandra."

"Oh, really? You're very particular about who you leave him with. Do I detect something blooming with your beautiful houseguest? I really like her, by the way."

He pulled into his parking spot behind the station. "Don't get too excited. She'll only be here for a month."

Her laugh echoed over the phone line. "I said the exact same thing. And look at me now. Married to the chief of police and loving my small-town life."

He hated that she was giving him hope where there was none. "Gotta go. I'll talk to you later."

He hung up before she could say more and dropped his forehead onto the top of his steering wheel. How would Cody react when it came time for her to go back to Manhattan? The child had already experienced such a huge loss, and now Luke had allowed him to get close to someone who'd be gone in a matter of weeks. Just as he was getting down on himself for poor parenting, he reminded himself that her presence was bringing his nephew out of his shell of sorrow. Fingers crossed he didn't revert once she was gone. He needed to have a serious conversation with Cody and explain that Alexandra would not be around forever.

I should explain that to myself.

He sat up straight and unbuckled his seat belt as an idea struck. He would use Mary Poppins as an example. She came to town, helped the Banks family and then went away. He would explain to his nephew that Alexandra really was like their very own Mary Poppins, and she would do the same. She'd leave when the time came. The conversation would be a breeze.

Not.

But he'd give it a try and hope for the best. He clocked in, said his morning hellos, checked his email and grabbed a set of keys to a patrol car. While driving his morning route around town, he had nothing to do but wave to citizens and think. And, of course, the thought on a repeated loop was his tempting houseguest. As eager as he'd been to get rid of her when she'd first arrived, there was really no reason for her to move to the hotel, other than his pitiful sleeping arrangements. Cody would balk at disassembling his bunk bed, but he could move the top mattress onto the floor, and it wouldn't matter so much if his feet hung off. He'd find a way to deal with his nephew's objections. Maybe Alexandra could turn it into a game and make it all better. Picturing her singing and dancing around the room put a smile on his face.

A better option would be slipping into his own king-size bed, tangling up with Alexandra and then sneaking back to his pallet on the floor before his nephew woke up. But friends with only partial benefits didn't sleep together, even if it was only snuggling. And single parents had to be extra cautious about their choices. Especially with someone who wasn't staying in town. Luke shook his head. There was no way in the universe he could share her bed and keep his kisses above the neck.

He sobered to the reality of his situation. In a matter of days, she'd slipped into their lives, enchanted Cody and charmed the ladies' man inside of him right out of hiding.

Two middle-school-aged boys ran down the sidewalk with cans of spray paint in each hand and ducked between the florist shop and hardware store.

Luke had noticed some graffiti popping up in a couple of locations and hated to think that these kids were the culprits. He pulled over and easily found them hiding behind a large wooden planter box. "Are you boys supposed to have that paint?"

Timothy Hargrove stood and stepped out of hiding. "No, sir."

"We're on our way to his parents' café," said the youngest of the Smith kids.

While giving both boys the standard officer stare, it occurred to him that Timothy was Alexandra's cousin. "Lucky for you, I'm going that way. I'll give you a ride." He waved them forward and chuckled at their hangdog expressions as they shuffled their feet on the way to his car.

Once the paint was stored in the trunk and the boys were in the back seat, they ducked down low enough not to be seen riding in the back of a police cruiser.

"How old are you two?"

"Twelve."

"You have to be eighteen to buy spray paint. How'd you two get it?"

One boy punched the other on the arm and they whispered between themselves. "We found it in my granddad's shed," Timothy said.

"Which one of you wants to tell me what you were planning to do with it?"

"I will," Timothy said. "Did you see that bad stuff spray-painted on the side of the old abandoned mill?"

"Are you telling me that was you two?"

"No way! We were planning to cover it up. It says something mean about a kid at our school who walks with braces on his legs."

"So you wanted to protect your friend?"

"Yes, sir," they said in unison.

A proud grin spread across Luke's face. He

pulled up around the corner from the café and turned to look at them. "I'd say that's an admirable reason. If I get the right kind of paint, how about we go cover it up together? Can you both meet me in front of the station at noon tomorrow?"

"I can," said the Smith kid.

"Me, too."

He climbed out of the car and opened the back door. "Stay out of trouble, you two."

"Thanks, Officer Walker." They took off running toward the café.

They were both good kids and he'd like to think he would've done the same kind of thing when he was their age. The rest of the morning went by slowly and without much excitement. A traffic stop for speeding, one warning for rolling through a stop sign and helping an older gentleman load his truck. Right before lunch, he was walking across the center of the town square as Alexandra and Cody came out of Mackintosh's Five and Dime with a big red-dragon kite. He quickened his steps and returned their waves. The midday sun glinted off Alexandra's hair, making her curls sparkle like rubies.

"Look, Uncle Luke. A kite, a kite, a kite," Cody said and held it up proudly.

"It's really cool, buddy." He caught Alexandra's gaze and they shared a smile.

She lifted both arms, revealing what had become her usual amount of shopping bags. "We've been to a few places around the square."

"We bought apples. We bought a bird feeder. We

bought art stuff." Cody spun in a slow circle, so the kite's tail trailed along the ground. "We bought a movie. A-a-and we bought a kite."

Luke couldn't believe how much he was talking. It both warmed his heart and made that little spark of jealousy flicker. "What movie did you get?"

"*Music Sound*," the little boy said.

"*The Sound of Music*," Alexandra clarified. "I thought since he likes *Mary Poppins* so much that he might like it."

"Fly it, Uncle Luke. Fly the kite."

On duty or not, he couldn't resist the request. Not to mention the wind had picked up to a perfect level, almost as if by magic. They followed the excited child into the open space in the park near the swings and flew the kite for a few minutes before the wind died down.

"Do you have time to eat with us?" she asked.

Luke glanced at his watch. "I need to stop at the station first. I'll meet y'all there in about fifteen minutes. Order me an iced tea, club sandwich and fries, please. And you better get a booth to make room for that big kite."

He headed across the park to the police station on the other side of the square, but couldn't resist glancing over his shoulder at Alexandra and Cody. His chest tightened with an emotion that he pushed aside before he had time to label it.

His shy, quiet nephew was taking to Alexandra like a flower leaning toward the sun. Could she help them grow and heal, or would she burn them with her brightness? Or, worse, leave them in darkness when she left?

Chapter Nine

Alexandra and Cody chose a large booth by the windows and waved to her uncle Sam in the kitchen. The shopping bags filled up half of one side and she squeezed in beside them. Cody and his kite took the other, leaving just enough room for his uncle.

A petite woman with shiny black hair curling around her shoulders came over to their table with menus. "Hello, Cody." She held out a hand to Alex. "I'm Sam's wife, Dawn. He told me you're the talented artist who painted the menu covers. Is it really okay if we make color copies?"

"Absolutely. I'd also be happy to paint a few more so you have choices."

"That would be wonderful. Just let me know what we owe you."

"I hadn't planned on charging you. I'll only be in town for a month and it's my gift to you for the Southern hospitality and delicious food." *And I'd love to be part of the family.*

"Well, then, you eat for free as long as you're in town. What can I get for you?"

"Luke will be joining us and wants an iced tea and club sandwich with fries. I'd like to try the chicken-fried steak and a Coke to drink. And not the diet stuff. In my short time here, I've become addicted to the real sugar version."

Cody's head popped up. "Addicted. A spoonful of sugar?"

"Probably way more than one. I don't even want to know how many spoons are in one bottle, but I'm on vacation and calories don't count."

Dawn chuckled. "I like your attitude. Cody, do you want your usual apple juice and chicken strip basket?"

"Chicken strips. French fries. Apple juice." The little boy tapped out each word on the edge of the table.

"Got it. I'll have your drinks out in a second." She wrote down their order and disappeared through the swinging door to the kitchen.

When her Coke arrived, Alex took a long drink and immediately ordered another.

A couple of minutes later, Luke slipped into the booth beside Cody and ruffled his hair. "I'm starving. Did you already order?"

"Yes, and I met Sam's wife," Alex said. "Do they have children?"

"One girl and one boy. I saw their son, Timothy, this morning. I caught him and another kid with spray paint and thought they were up to no good, but turns out, they were trying to protect a boy from their school. There's graffiti that makes fun of him for being different and they wanted to paint over it."

"Aww. Sounds like he's a good kid."

"Guess he comes from a good bloodline," he said and winked at her. "I'm not going into work tomorrow until early evening because I have to work the night shift. Several officers are sick and the one that was supposed to take the overnight is out of town with a broken-down car. I'm the only one available. Also, Anson reminded me that tomorrow night Cody has a ticket to go with him, Tess and Hannah to the Lego exhibit at the DoSeum Children's Museum in San Antonio."

Cody's head snapped up from his new book. "I like Legos."

"I know, buddy. You'll have a ton of fun, and then you'll spend the night with Hannah because it will be late when you get back, and I'll be at the police station all night. When I get home this evening, we'll pack your suitcase. Don't let me forget to put your noise-canceling headphones in your bag just in case it gets too loud at the museum."

A young waiter appeared with their food, and another Coke for Alex.

"Uncle Luke, Alexandra has sugar addicted. You should give her some sugar." The little boy said it loud enough for most of the café to hear.

Luke laughed just as he was trying to swallow a sip of iced tea and coughed. "Okay, buddy. Use your indoor voice, please."

When several people glanced their way and chuckled, Alex could feel her face flushing and changed the subject. "Turns out, Sam and Dawn really do want to use my painting for new menu covers. I told her I'd paint a few more so they have options."

"I'm not surprised. Could art become a career for you?"

Oh, boy, not the career discussion, again.

"You're very talented," Luke said.

"Thank you." His compliment took away some of the sting of him questioning her career choices, and she was glad she hadn't snapped at him to mind his own business. "I'm not sure I can make a career of my art, but I am waiting to hear about a music-therapist job at the Carrington Clinic in Manhattan. It's in the same building where my mom has her medical practice. I interviewed there the day before I came to Texas."

"And it's a job you want?"

"Absolutely. I'd get to work with kids and adults."

"Sounds like the perfect gig for you."

"Gig!" Cody said, and repeated it multiple times. She'd never admit it to Luke, but she was starting to become a little concerned about her future career track. Maybe it was him questioning her, or maybe it was just time to get a little more aggressive with her search. With there still being no word about her interview for the music-therapist position, it was probably time to move forward and look for other opportunities. Cooking was a skill she could always fall back on. She hadn't considered going back to being a nanny, but spending time with Cody had her considering it as a potential option.

Luke wiped ketchup from his nephew's cheek. "Alexandra, will you be okay at the house all alone tomorrow night?"

"I'm a big girl, and I'll be just fine."

"I'm a big boy," Cody said to Alexandra.

"Yes, you are, and I think you should help me try out the pie recipe when we get home."

"With a spoon of sugar?"

"A whole lot of spoons of sugar."

"What's the pie for?" Luke asked and pulled a toothpick from his club sandwich.

"I want to take something to the family dinner on Thursday and thought a pie might be a good option."

"Apple pie," Cody said with a french fry sticking out of the corner of his mouth.

"Lucky me. Hope I get to be a taste tester when I get home from work. I'll pay with extra sugar." He'd whispered the last few words so only she could hear him.

Just the thought of his lips on hers made her skin tingle. She kicked off one sandal under the table and traced her foot along his calf, grinning when he squeezed his sandwich and a tomato popped out. When they finished eating, Alex slipped out of the booth and started loading her arms with shopping bags. "Do you happen to have time to drive us home?"

Luke chuckled and took half of her load. "Yes. I'll drive you and your shopping bags home, again."

"I'll reward you later." She shivered when he flashed his full-watt smile. The one that made his eyes sparkle and one dimple appear at the corner of his mouth. And the way his gaze perused her body didn't feel the least bit uncomfortable. It made her forget all about telling him that the pie would be his prize…and consider offering something she shouldn't.

Luke hung his set of patrol-car keys in the cabinet and was more than ready to get home and relax. A shower, food and hanging out with Cody and Alexandra was just what he needed after a hot, sweaty afternoon of building the stage for the Fourth of July picnic.

"Walker, before you head home can we talk in my office?" Anson said.

"Sure." Not liking the worry on his friend's face, he followed and closed the door behind them before taking a seat. "What's up?"

The chief of police sat behind his desk and

rubbed both hands up and down his face. "I need you to keep this just between you and me for now. Money is missing from the charity fund that's supposed to go toward the Blue Santa program. Without it, I don't know how we'll provide all of the toys and stuff for needy families come December."

Wearing the blue velvet Santa suit and delivering toys had been one of the highlights of Luke's holiday last year, and he hated to think they couldn't repeat the needed program. "Any idea who could do such a thing?"

"Not yet, but the list is pretty short. I just made the discovery this afternoon. I'm looking into it and want you to keep your eyes and ears open." Anson's phone rang, and he looked at the caller ID. "I need to take this. Can we talk more tomorrow?"

"Sure thing. Have a good night." Luke left the office and headed for home.

After parking in the driveway, Luke walked around to the front of the house to check the mail. As he neared the front door, he could hear Cody singing, and when he stepped inside, Alexandra's voice drifted from the kitchen. They were both singing along with a song from *The Sound of Music*. How his nephew already knew the words, he had no idea. It was a new—and surprisingly emotional— experience to come home to his house filled with delicious scents of food cooking and the lively sounds of...a family.

A rush of something he wasn't sure he wanted

to identify flooded his chest and it both opened and tightened in the same moment.

"Hey, buddy. Do you like your new movie?"

"I like it," he said and then repeated the phrase in rapid succession while circling the coffee table.

His quiet, perfectly ordered—and sometimes lonely—bachelor pad had changed when his nephew moved in. But the appearance of a beautiful, mysterious free spirit made a drastic difference and took their environment to a whole new and interesting level. Her presence threw a spin into their world that he'd originally wanted no part of, but now, he wanted a lot more than he should. More than was safe.

She's only here temporarily. When she leaves...

He closed his eyes, reminding himself that getting too used to this domestic scene with *this* particular woman would be an epically bad idea. And letting Cody get too attached was not wise, but seeing his nephew happy once again was such a relief, he couldn't bear to take away the joy from him before he absolutely had to.

He'd start dating again and find the mother figure his nephew deserved, but not until *after* Alexandra went home to New York. Once it was just him and Cody, he'd also hire a nanny. Maybe Jenny, the babysitter that sometimes watched Hannah and Cody, would consider a full-time job at his house.

After hanging his hat on a hook by the door, he took in the whole space. The living room was surprisingly neat as a pin, and so was the dining room, but when he reached the kitchen door, it was a whole different scene. A disaster scene that might need to be roped off with yellow tape. The counters were covered with bowls and cooking implements that dripped with sticky goo. Red and green apple peels and flour were sprinkled across the table with scraps of dough, and the sink was stacked with a teetering pile of dirty dishes. Every burner of the stovetop held a pot that simmered with the promise of something tasty and made his stomach growl. He wanted to laugh at the outrageousness of it and cover his eyes at the same time. It was an Alexandra-style wreck. The kind where you wanted to look away but couldn't.

But the shock of the comic-like disaster fled his mind when she bent over to get something out of the oven, her nicely rounded bottom swaying to the beat of the music drifting in from the other room.

She placed a steaming pie on the only available spot on the counter and turned to smile at him. "Hey, there, Officer."

"I didn't startle you this time."

"I heard you talking to Cody. You have a deep voice that carries." She glanced around and bit the corner of her lip. "Are you going to arrest me for making a mess of your kitchen?"

He fingered the handcuffs on his belt and arched an eyebrow. "I'll let it slide this time, if you feed me. It smells great in here. Do I also smell coffee?"

"I made a pot. Want some?" Alex asked, and

continued bopping around the kitchen like a hyper squirrel.

He glanced at the coffee maker. "It's empty. Did you drink the whole pot?"

She stopped, glanced at the coffee maker, and then to her empty cup. "Hmmm, I guess I did. What time is it?"

"After six o'clock." Luke pulled a beer out of the refrigerator, twisted off the cap and sighed as the first cold sip hit his tongue, melting away a bit of the day's stress.

"What kind of beer is that?" she asked. "It's darker than the one you gave me before."

"It's Shiner Bock."

"Can I try it?"

"Sure. There's—" Before he could finish saying there were more in the refrigerator, she'd pulled the bottle from his hand. He watched in interested surprise as she put it to her mouth and tipped it up. Her satisfied moan, and the pink tip of her tongue slipping out to lick her lips, sent a bolt of fire straight to his groin. He swallowed hard as surprise turned to pure lust.

"That's actually good. I didn't think I liked beer, but maybe I do." She handed the bottle back and spun away to wash her hands.

He took another sip, hoping to taste the sweetness of her lips, and had never wanted to kiss her more than he did at this very moment. After setting the bottle aside, he stepped closer until his chest touched her back, his hands gripping the rim of the sink, trapping her against his body. "You promised a reward for driving you home."

Alexandra slowly turned and gazed up with a wicked gleam in her bright green eyes. "That's right. I did. I was planning to give you a piece of—" her top teeth caught the edge of her lower lip "—pie."

Her flirting hardened his body even more, and their breath mingled, drawing him deeper under her spell. His lips glided teasingly against hers, tasting cinnamon...and woman.

Cody's rapid footsteps across the dining room's creaky wooden floor warned of his approach, and they pulled apart before he darted into the kitchen. Luke's inner scream of disappointment could probably be heard a block away, and he needed to sit in an ice bath.

"Ready to eat?" Alexandra asked the little interrupter and fanned her flushed face.

"Pie? Apple pie?"

"Food first and then dessert," she said. "Let's clear off the table so we have somewhere to sit."

Cody slapped his hands to his cheeks. "Oh, no. Big mess. Big, big mess." He sat on the closest chair and covered his eyes.

"We can eat in the dining room," Luke suggested, while facing the counter to hide the physical state she'd put him in. "Amazingly, that table is clean."

Her hands snapped to her hips, and she shot him a scowl that transformed into a sheepish grin when she met his teasing smirk. "Good idea. I promise I'll get the kitchen spick-and-span right after we eat."

"Looks like you might be up late tonight. Good thing you drank all that coffee."

"Ha, ha. I can clean almost as fast as I can make a mess." She took three plates from the cabinet and started filling them with food.

He took a moment to concentrate on his old football stats, and work, and basically anything to get himself under control. "Around lunchtime tomorrow, I'm helping Timothy Hargrove and his friend paint over the graffiti. Do you want to come help?" Luke asked, and accepted the plate she'd filled with smothered chop steak, steamed broccoli and macaroni and cheese.

"Sure. What material is the wall made from?"

"It's plaster over cinderblocks."

"That would make a good canvas for a mural."

"We were just going to paint over it with white or something neutral." He held the plate out to Cody. "Hey, buddy, uncover your eyes and carry it with both hands, please. A mural is pretty ambitious."

"Ambitious." Cody repeated the word multiple times and carried his meal into the dining room.

"I know the perfect thing to paint. Tomorrow, we can prep the whole wall with a sky blue and get it ready for a woodland scene. I could paint lots of trees and a stream. Something to blend in with the natural environment."

They continued chatting about the mural as they

ate at the antique table, and Cody joined in on the conversation.

"Can you paint animals?" he asked her and climbed onto his knees to reach the saltshaker.

"Sure. How about squirrels, birds and a few deer?"

"Racoons, too," Cody said. "And a skunk."

Luke enjoyed their interaction but sighed inwardly. He and Alexandra had come to a point in their *friendship* where there was no turning back the clock. As much as he'd tried to bury his old nature, he couldn't be around her and not want it to be more between them. Time to give his self-discipline a good workout.

Once the chaos in the kitchen had been returned to order and Cody had been bathed and sung to sleep, Alexandra stood at the front porch railing and watched rain fall softly over the yard. Faraway lightning flickered from cloud to cloud and a low rumble of thunder rolled across the sky. She'd quickly grown to love the peace and quiet of this small town. She missed her mom and friends in the city, but letting herself fall into the rhythm of a slower pace was good for the soul.

The porch light went off, and at first, she thought the electricity had gone out. When she turned to the sound of the screen door's squeak, she saw the interior lights were still on. And just the sight of Luke made fireworks spark inside her.

He closed the screen but left the wooden door

open. "I need to be able to hear Cody if he calls for me. Sometimes thunder scares him."

"And you turned off the light because...?"

He stepped up beside her and wrapped an arm around her shoulders. "Privacy. I didn't get my full reward yet."

"You had a huge slice of pie." She encircled his waist and pressed against his big, warm body.

"And it was delicious, but I want something more. I'm craving your brand of sweetness. Seems I'm becoming a bit of a sugar addict myself."

"Well, then, I'm glad we decided to be friends with kissing benefits."

The sky illuminated, and lightning bolts reflected in his dark, moody eyes right before his lips devoured hers. Waves of tingles coursed across her skin, and she slid her hands under the back of his shirt as his tongue slipped past her lips. He tasted of apples and cinnamon, and his warm skin over hard muscle made her ache for more contact, and less clothes. No question, Luke knew how to kiss a woman senseless, and her mind eagerly spun with possibilities of other talents he likely possessed. But imagining his hands and mouth on other parts of her body was the only thing she could allow herself to do. She'd promised herself she would respect his situation, but he was making it a challenge and a half.

Luke nipped her lower lip and tugged it with his teeth. "Now that's my kind of reward. Where can I drive you tomorrow to earn another?"

As she opened her mouth to tell him he didn't

need to earn her kisses and could have one anytime, thunder boomed and rattled the windows. They both jumped and headed inside to the little boy who called out in fear.

Chapter Ten

Luke should have been sleeping to prepare for the night shift, but instead, he was at the hardware store He and Cody had loaded a shopping cart with paint trays, rollers and brushes, but Alexandra still stood at the paint counter getting the correct shade of blue mixed for the base coat of the mural.

Dr. Clark came up beside them. "Hello, Cody. How's your day, Walker?"

"It's going well."

"I think you remember my niece, Gwen?" He motioned to the woman behind him. "After a bit of a delay, she finally arrived in town yesterday."

"Yes, it's nice to see you again." In a matter of days, Luke had forgotten he'd told the old doctor that he'd be more than happy to take his niece out on a date. Before Luke could hold out a hand to Gwen, he received an enthusiastic hug from the petite woman, and she didn't seem inclined to let go, clinging to him like an enamored female. And, of course, that was the very moment Alexandra turned to put two buckets of paint into her cart. She flashed a surprised expression before quickly turning away to talk to the man behind the counter.

Awkward.

Gwen Clark was even prettier than he remembered, and exactly the type of woman he would have gone for once upon a time, but he felt nothing for her. No attraction in the least. He finally pried himself loose from her grasp. "I understand you'll be joining your uncle at his medical practice?"

"That's right. I've been looking forward to getting out of the city and settling in Oak Hollow." She held out a hand to Cody. "Hello there. How are you today?"

His nephew clung to his leg and ducked his head. "He's shy around new people."

"That's okay. We'll have plenty of time to get to know one another."

"Walker," Dr. Clark said. "I've decided to retire, hopefully by the end of the year."

"Oh, that's a surprise." This was not good news. He was the only doctor Cody had ever had, and he trusted the man. He shifted his gaze to Gwen. "I thought you were a nurse and didn't realize you were a doctor."

"I'm a nurse practitioner. We'll be looking for a new doctor to help me run the practice."

Alexandra pushed the heavy cart toward the front register, and she took the long way around, probably to avoid passing by him and the Clarks.

"I hope we have more time to talk soon, but we need to get going. I have some people waiting for me at the police station."

They said their goodbyes and he and Cody met Alexandra at the register. "The city is paying for these supplies since the mill has become city property." He filled out the check and thanked the cashier.

Cody climbed into her cart and sat on a paint can for a ride through the parking lot. At the truck, he got into the back seat with a bag of paintbrushes and used two of them as drumsticks against the back of the front seat.

"How did you get a city purchase like this approved in only a few hours?" she asked, finally breaking her rare moment of silence.

"I called the mayor. She was excited about the project and said to move forward with it."

"You must have a lot of sway with the mayor." She put a can of paint into the bed of his truck beside the ladder.

"I know her pretty well. We go way back."

"You certainly do have a way with women."

He cringed but also wanted to smile like the Cheshire cat. She was jealous. If she only knew that the mayor was old enough to be his grandmother.

When they pulled up in front of the police station, there were a whole lot more than the two pre-teen boys he'd expected. It made him proud of his town to see six children and three parents waiting to help cover up the graffiti. "See the blond-haired little boy with the blue striped T-shirt?" He leaned close to her ear so Cody couldn't hear. "That's your cousin Timothy Hargrove. Sam's son."

"Oh, wow. Cute kid. Is his sister here?"

"I don't see her. Wait here and I'll see if every-one can follow us over to the old mill."

Alex positioned herself near her cousin Timothy while they painted and casually chatted. She asked him about school, hobbies and if he had any sib-lings. He was very forthcoming about his older sis-ter, who was way too into boys and makeup. He was animated, gesturing with his hands and dripping paint on his clothes as he talked, and she couldn't help but wonder if he looked anything like her fa-ther had at the same age.

After a few hours, the wall was a sky blue that covered up the graffiti. It had become the perfect blank canvas for the mural she envisioned. Alex talked with the children to get their suggestions for the artwork. They all liked her woodland-scene idea and put in their thoughts on details that should be hidden in the scene. Faces worked into the bark of a tree. Little animals peeking out of holes. And one of the girls wanted tiny fairies dancing among the leaves, something Alex totally agreed with.

"Are you an art teacher?" asked Mrs. Smith, one of the parents.

"No, I'm not. I don't have a teaching certificate."

"You should get one. If you have a college degree, you can get an alternative certification. I'm the superintendent of the Oak Hollow schools, and I know there's an opening for an art teacher at the middle school coming up in August. And you're really good with the kids."

"Thank you. I'll certainly keep that in mind."

Luke heard the compliment and winked at Alex. "She's also a musician."

"Oh, really?" Mrs. Smith's smile widened. "There's an opening for a music teacher at the elementary school."

The compliment and job suggestions set off new ideas. She hadn't considered becoming a teacher, and as much as she was enjoying working with the kids, she added it to her list of possibilities.

Once everything was cleaned up, Alex rode with Luke to take Cody over to Anson's for his trip to the Lego exhibit. The Curry family home was an amazing three-story white Victorian with gorgeous landscaping and a huge front porch perfect for sitting. They were greeted at the door by Anson's delightful grandmother, who everyone in town called Nan. With her white hair in an elegant bun and an open, friendly smile, Alex knew this was a woman she would like.

"Please, come inside. I've been looking forward to meeting you," Nan said, and led them into a front formal living room filled with antique furnishings and old family photos. "Jenny has made some absolutely precious clothes for the kids to wear on their outing today. Excuse me while I go and get her."

Cody took a seat at a piano in one corner of the room and started practicing some of the scales she'd taught him on the keyboard.

"He's picking up everything I teach him so quickly. You really should think about getting a piano," she said to Luke.

"Until I do, I'm sure Nan won't mind if he practices on hers."

A minute later, a young woman with dark hair that hung in long waves past her waist walked into the room. "Hello, everyone. Cody, I didn't know you could play the piano."

"Alexandra teaches me," he yelled over his shoulder without stopping or turning around.

Luke put a hand on the small of Alex's back. "Jenny, this is Alexandra. She's visiting from Manhattan."

"Nice to meet you," Alex said, and admired the halter-style maxi dress the other woman was wearing.

"You, too. Have you always lived in New York City?"

"Yes. Born and raised there."

"I would love to visit the city. There's a fashion design school that I'd like to attend. Someday." Jenny sighed and glanced at her feet.

"Then you'll have to come and visit me once I return home. I can show you all around town."

"That would be wonderful."

Hannah bounced into the room with her usual amount of energy and twirled, making her skirt flair and ripple around her little legs. "Look at my new dress."

"It's beautiful," Alex exclaimed, and she bent to look closely at the material covered with colorful images of toys. "This is adorable. You made this?" she asked Jenny.

"I did, and I made a matching shirt for Cody to wear." Jenny crossed the room and handed the folded button-up to the little boy.

"Thank you." He got up from the piano bench and shook it open, studied the material and began naming the toys.

"Let me help you put it on." Luke kneeled to help his nephew.

"You're very talented," Alex said. "I've yet to attempt sewing. Did you just follow a pattern?"

"I did for Cody's shirt, but I made the pattern for the dress."

"Wow. You should definitely follow your passion and pursue fashion. Did you also make the dress you're wearing?"

"I did." Jenny held out the skirt and the material, which looked as if it had been painted with watercolors, flowed in a silky wave. "I can make one for you, and you can even pick out the fabric."

"That would be amazing. A dress like that would sell for a high price in Manhattan."

Nan returned and sat on a maroon velvet sofa. "Looks like you two girls have become instant friends."

"I think you're right," Luke agreed. "They have a lot in common with their artistic abilities."

Tess rushed into the room with a pair of strappy sandals in her hand and sat beside Nan. "Hello, everyone. Sorry I'm running late. I lost track of time while I was researching antiques for Mr. Gibb. Anson is getting dressed and will be down in a minute."

After the three young women made plans for a girls' night out, Tess, Anson and the kids set off on their adventure to the San Antonio children's museum.

In the truck on the way back to Luke's house, he reached across the center console and tugged gently on one of her curls. "You seem to fit right in wherever you go. Everyone likes you immediately."

Alex laughed, remembering how he'd acted toward her when she'd first arrived in town. "Everyone except you. Or have you forgotten how you needled me at every possible turn?"

"I might have been trying to resist my attraction and keep you at a distance. What do you plan to do tonight with the house all to yourself?"

"I might work on some music or a new painting." She held up her hand and studied her nails. "Maybe watch a Hallmark movie and paint my nails. You know, super exciting stuff."

"You're a wild one," he teased, and laced his fingers with hers.

If he was staying home, she'd show him what a wild one she could be.

After a few very slow hours at the police station, Luke drove home, locked his truck and headed for his front door. The porch light was on, but the inside of the house appeared dark, and he really hoped Alexandra was still awake. Since Officer Carter had shown up at ten thirty with a repaired car, ready to take the rest of his night shift, he'd been thinking of nothing but spending time alone with her—without the possibility of a child's interruption. He turned his key in the lock and stepped into his dark living room.

"Crap." Luke caught hold of the couch just in time to keep himself from face-planting two steps inside of his front door.

What the hell did I trip on?

He flipped on the light and kicked aside a pair of wedge sandals, then pulled his hand from where it had landed, in the full laundry basket. A red lacy bra dangled from his wristwatch. So this was the sexy stuff hiding under her flowy tops. He untangled the bra and barely resisted bringing it to his nose to see if it held her herbal scent. He took in the rest of the room and groaned. The coffee table he liked to keep cleared—except for the remote controls and Cody's timer—was strewn with bottles of nail polish, an open fashion magazine and colored pencils.

"Damn. It's a female takeover."

A trail of beauty bread crumbs led to a silk scarf draped over the built-in room divider, sheets of hand-written music blanketing his grandmother's dining-room table and watercolor paints and paper scattered across the kitchen table. She'd once again made a mess on every available surface.

Just before he called out for her, a painting of Cody caught his eye. She'd managed to capture the way he felt about his nephew, and the vulnerability in the young boy's eyes went straight to his heart. There was a second one of them walking down the sidewalk, each with a hand tucked in their back pocket. His moment of irritation softened, especially when her singing caught his attention and drew him down the hallway. He followed the sound of her voice until he stood outside the bathroom… where she was taking a shower. An image of her naked with her soft skin all wet, slick with soap and…

He jerked his hand off the doorknob and shook his head. "Get it together, dude."

Even though he'd come home with the intentions of possibly breaking the friends-with-only-kissing-benefits arrangement they had agreed on, he couldn't just barge into the shower and assume she wanted the same. He rushed past to his bedroom but found no relief from her enticing scent and unusual charms. His room looked as if there'd been an explosion of floral prints, tie-dye, denim and sexy lingerie.

He laughed at the outrageousness of the whole scene and then turned and strode back down the hallway just as she opened the bathroom door.

Alexandra collided with him, screamed and braced her palms on his chest. And dropped her towel. Rather than picking it up, she pressed herself tighter against his body. "Luke Walker, you scared the hell out of me. Again. What are you doing home?"

"I…" He couldn't think, much less form words with the soft, damp skin of her back under his hands as her bare body molded to the front of his. From this moment on, every time he looked at his uniform shirt, he'd picture the soft swells of her breasts straining upward with the force of their embrace. Begging to be caressed. To be kissed.

To be his.

If he eased away just the slightest bit, he could discover the color of the nipples that he'd seen peaked under the thin fabric of her lacy bra and T-shirt. He squeezed his eyes closed and finally managed to speak. "The other officer showed up for his shift."

"Is Cody here?" she asked, her voice going husky.

"No."

Bless Anson and Tess for that!

Her death grip on his shirt eased, and she splayed her fingers over his pecs, her lips curving up and eyes glowing with invitation. "We're alone?"

"All night." His mouth hovered just above hers, close enough that he could almost taste the mint of her toothpaste. "All. Night. Long."

Alexandra moaned and kissed him softly, leisurely swirling her tongue with his and turning his blood to molten fire. He shivered and every hair stood at attention.

With her arms twined around his neck, she raised onto her toes and put her lips against his ear. "You should get out of this uniform. One of your weapons is digging into my belly."

He chuckled, desperately glad they were on the same page, and slid his hands down to cup her hips, pulling her more firmly against him. "That's not something I can take off. That's all me, sweetheart. See what you do to me?"

It was her turn to shiver, her breasts rubbing against the rough fabric of his uniform shirt, causing a gasp and her eyes to light with passion. Luke dipped his head and took her mouth in a deep kiss. Tongues tangling and sweeping. Sparring and retreating. Urgently. And so sweetly.

"Alexandra, I want you. I want more. Kissing isn't enough. But I won't do anything you're not comfortable with."

"Luke. Ple-e-e-ase."

Her voice was barely audible, but he felt her need to the depths of his bones. "What do you need, sweetheart? Tell me and I'll do it."

"Take me to bed, cowboy." She clamped her teeth on his chin then soothed it with her lips. "Please."

When she stepped back, he caught his breath and his blood ran suddenly hotter. The shower steam and hazy light filtering from the bathroom cast her in an ethereal glow. Her body was flushed from hot water, and she was even more beautiful than he'd imagined, with a small tree-of-life tattoo on her hip. He had the strong urge to place a kiss right on top of it.

She trailed her fingers along his arm and brushed past him on her way to the bedroom, and then the temptress glanced over her shoulder with a grin that almost put him on his knees. After a second of foolishly standing there in a dazed stupor, he made it to the open door in time to see her crawl onto the bed. The woman of his dreams stretched out on her side, her long hair falling forward, covering her breasts, and one leg slightly bent to hide her most private parts. Backlit by the closet light, enticing shadows painted her bare skin, reminding him of priceless art.

He'd never seen anything so erotic.

Not wanting to take his eyes off her for a second more than necessary, he quickly unholstered his weapon and locked it in the safe, and then returned to her while unbuttoning his shirt. "You are so beautiful."

She climbed onto her knees, tugged him forward by a belt loop and started unfastening his pants while kissing his chest. Between the two of them, he was down to black boxer briefs in no time. When she pressed her body against his, skin-to-skin, he hissed and grasped her full bottom, squeezing her soft flesh.

She trembled and arched, pressing her hips more firmly against his, silently asking for what she wanted, and moaned as if she'd gotten the pressure just right. "I've never been so turned on."

Her confession stroked his ego and heightened his own arousal. With her body tilted back, he cupped the under swells of her breasts, filling his palms, lifting the weight and sliding his thumbs over rosy nipples beaded and begging to be soothed by his tongue. He did exactly that as he eased her onto the mattress, sucking a tight bud between his lips.

"Ohhh, yes." Her eyes closed, and she cradled his head. "Please, don't stop touching me."

"Not a chance, sweetheart." He loved the way her fingers tugged his hair, and she was so responsive, so ready. So beautifully sexy. If he pulled off his boxer briefs, he might not resist, and he needed to please her first. "I plan to make you moan all night long."

"I've wanted you like this since the moment I saw you at the town square."

It was nothing new to have a woman tell him she wanted him, but something about this time was very different. And he couldn't put his finger on exactly what it was, but hearing it from Alexandra sent a shot straight to his heart. How had he let this happen? He'd opened himself to her more than any other woman he'd ever been with.

"I almost asked if you needed a ride that same day, but I was afraid I'd do this." He trailed his fingers along her collarbone then slowly across one breast. While his hand continued on a slow path to the dip of her waist, and around to the swell of her bottom, he kissed a path lower and lower. Her pleasure became his, and fire raced through him as he began a slow, teasing pace, and she whispered his name.

Luke startled himself with his urgency to connect, and the fact that he thought of this not as just sex, but as making love.

Chapter Eleven

The lights were low, the passion off the charts, and the air sparked with electricity that tingled across her skin. When Luke's fingers grazed along her inner thigh, Alex opened for him, completely willing to see where this ride took them. Who in their right mind could really expect a girl to stop under these circumstances? The house all to themselves. A very aroused cowboy staring at her like he would eat her up at any second. And enough heat between them to spark a blaze hot enough to melt sand into glass. Fitting, since he was caressing her as if she was as fragile as fine crystal, although she knew he was as hard as stone.

His fingers glided across her skin, featherlight and achingly slow, before his warm palm cupped her, pressing just hard enough to make all coherent thoughts scatter. A current pulsed down to her toes and then rushed back up to settle under his hand. She arched against him, seeking everything he had to offer, which turned out to be a wide array of talents. Slow, teasing circles, quick flicks and a long, slow pull of suction right where she needed it to shatter. A warm wave of sensation bathed her with pleasure and her world tilted on its axis, her daydreams about this sexy man becoming a reality in a more spectacular fashion than she could've imagined. Once her breath and vision returned, she opened her eyes as he slid up her body and stretched out beside her.

"Wow." That was the only word that came to mind. She rolled to drape her leg across his and stroked the curve of his face, returning his satisfied smile. The man could do wickedly delicious things, and finding out what other tricks he had to share sounded like a winning idea.

"You're so sweet," he whispered. "So responsive to my touch. Watching the pleasure on your face is a huge turn-on."

His kiss was tender, although with the tension and tremble of his body, she knew he was desperate for his own release, and amazingly, a lovely pressure was already building in her own. They were doing something she'd told herself she wouldn't, but at the moment it felt right. So right and so natural. Once she returned to Manhattan, the memory of this night would forever be hers to pull out and relive at will.

Alex dipped her hand lower, and just at his navel… *Oh, my, hello, cowboy.* She tugged down his boxer briefs, loving the power of him shuddering, groaning against her shoulder and then nipping with his teeth.

His eager touch glided from the nape of her neck, spreading a trail of fire along her spine and tugging her more firmly against his arousal.

"Alexandra, wait." His voice was a rough whisper, forced through a clenched jaw. "Your touch… So-o-o good."

She wrapped her arms around his neck, giving him a moment, but she couldn't deny being thrilled to have this effect on him. "Officer Luke Walker, you said you'd do what I needed, and so far, you've delivered with blazing colors. And now, I need *all* of you."

His cocky grin appeared. "Your wish is my command, sweetheart." He reached into the bedside table drawer but didn't take his eyes off her.

His heated gaze was enough to spike her already off-the-charts desire. Skin sensitive and every nerve ending sparking, she was so eager to share this moment with Luke. It had been a long while since she'd been with a man, and there hadn't been that many to begin with, but he made her feel like the most powerful and sexy woman on earth. Would he sense her boldness was only an act? A show to make him believe she was experienced? This confidence was something only Luke had ever brought out in her with his smoldering gaze, honeyed words and an expert touch that set her ablaze.

When he settled between her legs with a body that looked as if it had been sculpted of warm stone, she arched her hips, craving all of him, but he moved achingly slow, even though the tension in his jaw made it obvious he was barely restraining himself. With her legs wrapped around his hips, she pulled him closer.

"I don't want to hurt you, sweetheart."

"You won't hurt me. I'm aching for you."

"I'll make it better." He cupped her cheek and kissed her deeply as he shifted his hips, eliciting a shared moan.

She fell headlong into their consuming passion, seeking everything he had to offer and giving all in return. When she cried out, he threw back his head and followed her.

Tangled in the afterglow, she explored the dips and curves of this beautifully built man who'd just rocked her world. "I knew in a New York minute you'd be a good lover."

He chuckled. "A New York minute?"

"Yep. The second you strutted across the street with a bag of ice over one shoulder." She probably shouldn't be stroking his already large ego, but she was just being honest.

"I don't strut."

She laughed at his shocked tone. "Whatever you say, cowboy. I'm not complaining one little bit."

Alex snuggled deeper in his embrace and kissed his neck. "I like watching you walk around in your jeans *and* your uniform."

"I like watching you walk around in nothing at all."

When Alex woke before dawn, warm, naked and entwined in Luke's embrace, she carefully tilted her head and cracked one eye open. He was sleeping peacefully, his handsome face shadowed with dark stubble and relaxed in slumber, making him look younger than his twenty-eight years. A bit vulnerable yet strong at the same time. She couldn't resist tracing the line of his jaw and down along his neck to his chest, dusted with a few dark hairs in all the right spots. Goose bumps rose on his skin.

It was *the morning after*, and one never quite knew what to expect. Especially when their night hadn't been planned. Quite the opposite. Desire had consumed them, and in her mind, sex had turned into lovemaking, both frantic with passion and tenderness.

And absolutely, no doubt, hands down the best sexual experience of her life.

But would he feel the same or regret their night together when he woke? Should she slip out of bed before then? She put aside that thought immediately. Cody wasn't home and this might be her only chance to enjoy the comfort of Luke's arms, and the intoxicating scent of his skin, warmed with desire and passion. She kissed his chest, and just as she closed her eyes to try to go back to sleep, his arm tightened around her, drawing her closer.

"Alexandra, I want you again." His voice was deep and gravelly with sleep.

Instant, sharp arousal burned through her blood, and without a word, she straddled his waist and took control.

Hazy morning light filtered through the blinds, and although he'd barely slept, Luke felt energized. He stroked the length of Alexandra's smooth back as she lay curled against his side, one arm and leg draped across his body, pinning him to the bed in a very agreeable way. Trapping him physically. And emotionally.

Damn. I'm done for. She's stolen my willpower and ruined me.

"So…we kind of broke our rules," she said and kissed his shoulder.

"Kind of?" He chuckled, enjoying the slide of her soft, bare skin against his. "Kind of three times."

"How did we let this happen?"

Rolling her onto her back, he braced himself above her. "First, we shattered the no-kissing-below-the-neck rule, like this." He slid his lips across her collarbone and worked his way down to the swell of her breasts, loving the way her nails dug in to his shoulders as she urged him closer.

"And then," she said while wrapping her legs around his waist, "remind me what happened next. Tell me about the second rule we broke."

"Sweetheart, we broke *all* the rules, proving neither of us has any willpower where the other is concerned." The way she held his gaze and the tenderness of her fingers running through his hair struck a place in his heart that he rarely visited, quickening its pace. And making him momentarily forget everything outside of their contented bubble.

"What should we do now? Do we…?" She sighed and bit the corner of her lower lip. "Do we have to set new rules?"

"I hate rules," he growled and nipped her earlobe, making her squirm under him, setting off a new round of sparks. Her laughter heightened his happiness.

"But you're a peace officer. You're supposed to be all about the rules and following them to the letter of the law."

"In ninety-nine percent of my life I do, but when it comes to being alone with you…" He kissed the valley between her breasts. "You've created a felon. I want to be a wicked criminal if it means spending time alone with you."

"Officer by day and rule breaker by night?"

"Will you keep my secret?" He caressed her leg from ankle to hip.

"Luke, was this a onetime thing that only happened because Cody wasn't here?"

"Do you want it to be?"

"No. But I'll do whatever you think is best for your situation. Cody needs to come first."

Her concern for his nephew was a beautiful

thing, and it meant a lot to him. "I'm not sure there can be rules when it comes to things like this between us, but I know I don't want this to be a one-time deal."

"We are single, consenting adults."

"Exactly. Since you're only here temporarily, what do you say we agree to enjoy the time we have together and then part as friends who shared some really fantastic benefits?"

"That's a fabulous idea."

"We'll just have to be careful about how we go about things around Cody."

"Sneaking around could add a bit of spice."

He hooked an arm under her knee. "Will you show me the perks of our new arrangement? And add a little sugar to the spice?"

She answered with a kiss, her body trembling under his hands and setting off a full-body shiver that sent his blood southward.

Chapter Twelve

Alex had taken extra time with her hair and makeup and changed clothes three times before finally deciding on a blue '50s-style dress with a boat-neck collar and a pair of red leather flats. Now, it was finally time for her first family dinner at her grandparents' home. With an apple pie in her lap, they drove past the square to the most prestigious area of town. Cody had become agitated by the sound of a jackhammer when they stopped at a red light and had put on his noise-canceling headphones. She needed some calming herself and focused on Luke singing along with the radio. When he smiled, a delicious shiver raced through her body, sparking memories of last night and settling her nerves.

Luke pulled up in front of a large redbrick colonial-

style house with white columns flanking the front
door and black shutters. The picture-perfect landscaping was too structured for her taste but well-
tended. Evenly spaced, meticulously trimmed
bushes lined the circular front drive, where a lux-
ury car, a Jeep and a truck were parked.

"I wonder how many people are here?" she said.

"From the looks of it, everyone is here. Are you
nervous?"

"A bit." When she made no move to open her
door, he took her hand, and she was thankful he
knew the truth and was there to support her.

"You look beautiful, and they're going to adore
you. Try to relax and enjoy getting to know them.
Then you can decide when to reveal your identity."

"I've been waiting for this for so long, and now,
I'm excited and scared to death at the same time.
But you're right. I just need to take a breath and get
to know everyone."

"I think Audrey is the president of the garden
club. She'll get a kick out of you trying to improve
my sad yard. So that's something you can talk to
her about." Luke turned to Cody in the back seat
and motioned for him to take off his headphones.
"Time to go inside."

She stepped down from the running board and
then reached in for the pie and carried it with trembling hands.

Her uncle Sam's wife, Dawn, opened the door.
"Welcome. It's so nice to see you again. Come on
inside."

"Thank you." The elegant marble-floored entry opened into a living room, and Alex could see family photos on the walls. Just what she'd been hoping for to start a conversation that might yield information about her father.

"Whatever that is you brought smells delicious."

"Apple pie," Cody said to Dawn.

"Yummy. Did you help bake it?"

"Yep. With sugar." The little boy turned away from them and headed toward the two kids who waved and called him over.

"Those are my children, Mary and Timothy. They're watching some new animated movie."

"I met your son yesterday when we were painting out at the mill."

"That's right. He told me all about the mural. Sounds like it's going to be amazing."

Luke and Alex followed Dawn into the kitchen. Seeing her very own grandmother at the stove stirring a pot of beans seemed like such a normal, everyday activity, but for Alex, it was a real treasure.

"Good evening. So happy y'all could make it," Audrey said.

"I'm glad to be here. I appreciate being included in your family dinner." Alex placed the covered pie on the counter and tried not to be obvious as she took in every detail of the kitchen, from Viking appliances to marble surfaces and antique touches. "I hope it's okay that I brought an apple pie."

"Absolutely. It will be the perfect ending to the barbecue."

Timothy stuck his head around the corner of the kitchen doorway. "Officer Walker, can I talk to you?"

"Sure thing. If you ladies will excuse me, please." He followed the boy out of the room.

"Can I help you with anything?" she asked her grandmother.

"Everything is pretty much done in here, but if you girls would take those trays of drinks and snacks to the table in the backyard, I'd appreciate it. The men are outside at the grill."

"Sure." Alex grabbed a tray of cheese, crackers and fruit, then followed Dawn through the house.

An older gentleman in a golf shirt opened the sliding glass door and gave her a curious stare. "Hello, young lady. I'm William Hargrove."

My grandfather!

She was glad for the snack tray because she might've hugged him if her hands had been free. Did he remember her mother enough to see the resemblance? "It's a pleasure to meet you. I'm Alex."

"Make yourself at home." He swiped a piece of cheese off her tray and grinned. "Excuse me while I go prep the steaks."

She put her tray on the glass-topped patio table that overlooked a shady backyard with a pool to the left and a trampoline off to the right.

"I'm going to go tell the kids to get out from in front of the television," Dawn said.

Sam waved from the far side of the pool, where he was scooping leaves with a long-handled net.

He shook the net into the grass and then headed toward the garage.

A tall man with broad shoulders and long, tanned arms stood at the grill. He had a strong profile with a short but full blond beard and looked to be in his late forties. She crossed the stone patio to say hello and see if he was another family member.

The man turned at her approach, and his broad smile fell away as his mouth dropped open. A beer bottle slipped from his grasp, shattering on the flagstones, and he clasped a hand to his chest.

She rushed forward and grabbed his arm, fearing he was having a heart attack. "Are you okay? Should I call for help?"

"No." He rubbed a hand across his mouth. "No. I'm okay. I just… I thought you were someone else for a second. Striking resemblance."

People always remarked how much she looked like her mother. Something clicked. A stirring inside her. A hope—that couldn't possibly be true—flitted through her mind. Still grasping his bicep, she studied his blue-gray eyes that had a slight upward tilt at the outer corners. She flashed to the photographs of her father that had always hung on the wall. They'd been her mother's attempt to make sure she knew she had a father who would have loved her.

"Who did you think I was?" she asked, her throat tight and tears paused at the ready. Could her wild hope actually be true?

His smile was sad, and his eyes took on a faraway gaze as if reliving a precious memory. "I knew her many years ago. Her name was Kate."

Her heartbeat thudded painfully at the base of her throat and blood whooshed in her ears. "What...? What's your name?" She held her breath, again predicting the answer.

"Charlie."

The choked sound that escaped her lips was part whimper, part gasp. "You're Charles Alexander Hargrove?"

His gaze snapped to her face, and he studied her intently. "That's right. How'd you know? Who are you?"

Alex's vision blurred and it was her turn to need smelling salts like a swooning Southern belle.

"Whoa," he said, and put an arm around her waist as her knees buckled.

Luke was suddenly beside them and swooped her up into his arms. "Alexandra, are you okay?"

She buried her face against Luke's neck and clung to him. "I don't know. I don't understand what's happening."

He carried her over to a bench and sat her down, then took the spot beside her. "Just breathe, sweetheart. Tell me what has you so upset."

Charlie followed and kneeled on one knee in front of them. "You're her daughter, aren't you?"

After covering her face and counting to three, she met her father's eyes. "Yes. Kate is my mother."

This revelation was so completely beyond anything she thought she'd discover, and she hadn't been prepared for this outcome. Never could've predicted it. How could she honor her mother's request and wait to tell him?

Charlie stared into space like he was watching a memory play out before him. "I loved that woman with all my heart. And then she broke mine."

"How are you alive?" Alex blurted out. "I thought you died in Belize."

"I almost did. I was badly injured in an accident. When I got home, my Katie had married someone else." His jaw clenched. "To your father, I assume?"

Bewilderment heaped on top of confusion, and she didn't know what to say. Was this reality or had she been thrust into a hallucination?

Sam had come out of the garage and was glancing between them with his eyebrows knitted. "What's wrong? What's going on?"

No one answered him, because no one knew.

Lines of tension formed around her father's wounded blue eyes, deepening a faded scar that ran along the side of his face.

"My mother has never been married."

"What? Wait." Charlie sprang to his feet, his voice rising in volume. "Does Kate think I'm dead?"

She left the comfort of Luke's side and stood in front of her father. "Yes, she does." Before she could ask how this had happened, he paced away. The gray fabric of his cotton button-up pulled tight across his back as he tensed his arms and fists.

He spun to face her and pressed the base of his palms hard against his eyes. "No, no, no. The authorities got me mixed up with another man. For a few weeks, my family thought I was dead. My mother told me she'd talked to Kate several times, and that she'd married someone else. That she knew I was home but was too embarrassed to talk to me." He sucked in a sharp breath and put a shaking hand against her cheek. "How old are you?"

"I'm twenty-five. And…" With her hand over the top of his, she smiled. "I'm your daughter."

An incoherent sound escaped him, and he pulled her into his arms. "You're mine? My baby?" He kissed the crown of her head. "Oh, my God. I have a child with my Katie. I have a daughter." His voice was choked with so much emotion it had become a husky whisper.

Being in her father's strong embrace for the first time overwhelmed her, and tears streamed down her cheeks. He smelled faintly of soap and woodsmoke from the grill. If this was a hallucination, she wanted to stay in fantasyland. "How could this mistake happen? Why would your mother think my mom got married?"

Charlie held her by the shoulders and slowly shook his head. "That's a damn good question, and I intend to find out."

When he stepped away from her, Sam grabbed his arm. "Wait, brother. Take a minute. There are a lot of people here. The children. Don't make a scene in front of the children."

Charlie jerked his arm away from Sam. "Did you know about this?"

"Hell, no. This is all news to me, too, big brother."

"Somebody has some major explaining to do. And I think we both know who to start with." Charlie turned on his boot heel then stood still, hands flexing, looking every bit like a man planning a mission.

Luke wrapped his arms around Alex from behind and leaned forward to kiss her cheek. "Breathe, sweetheart. It'll be okay."

His support and comfort were more appreciated than he could know, and she laced her fingers through his. "I can't believe this. What should I do now?"

Before he had a chance to answer, the three children ran outside and headed for the trampoline in the corner, followed by her grandparents. The ones who hopefully had explanations for this unbelievably tragic mix-up.

Charlie stalked forward and pointed at his parents. "You two, inside. Now." His voice was pitched low and sounded somewhat menacing.

"Boy, you might be grown, but you still need to watch your tone," his father said.

Charlie ignored the rebuff and stormed through the back door. Sam took his parents by the arms and led them to follow, passing his startled wife as she crossed the patio.

"Let's get Cody and leave," Luke said.

Alex shook her head and stepped out of his embrace. "No. I can't. You can go if you need to get him out of here, but I need to know the whole truth."

"I'm not leaving you, sweetheart."

"What in the world is happening?" Dawn asked.

"Luke will explain while you two keep the children outside, please." When Alex stepped into the house, she followed the raised voices to a wood-paneled office. Her father and uncle stood on one side of the room and her grandparents on the other beside a large, mahogany desk in front of a wall of books.

"I'm sorry, but this is a private family matter," her grandmother said.

Charlie wrapped an arm around Alex's shoulders and pulled her in against his side. "Yes, it *is* a family matter, *Mother*."

"Oh, my God." Her grandfather sat down hard in his desk chair. "You're our granddaughter, aren't you? You look just like her."

Audrey Hargrove made a pained sound and clasped her hands in front of her mouth. "I didn't know. Why didn't she tell us she was pregnant?"

Charlie let go of Alex and stepped closer to his parents, glaring straight at his mother. "Because she thought I was dead! Why did she think that? Was it all your idea, or was Dad in on it, too?"

"Me?" William sputtered, then paused a moment before he could form coherent words again. "I thought Kate had run off and married someone else. I thought she'd broken my boy's heart. That's what…" His hard stare snapped to his wife, and he inhaled deeply. "Audrey, was that true? Did Kate tell you she'd gotten married?"

She sat on the edge of the desk and looked at her husband with haunted eyes.

"Audrey, what did you do?" he asked his wife.

"I thought it was for the best." She wrung her hands, shoulders curling in as if she could hide. "You wanted Charlie to come home, go to law school and take over your practice here in Oak Hollow. I thought it was just puppy love between him and Kate and he'd move on and fall in love for real with someone here in town. I thought maybe he'd go back to his high-school girlfriend."

The room was deathly quiet as everyone tried to process her words and the unbelievable situation she'd put them in. The many lives she'd altered. The years and memories she'd stolen.

Alex backed up until she bumped into the wall. Framed degrees and awards rattled against the dark wood and blood whooshed in her ears. This whole situation was surreal. As raw as she felt, she couldn't begin to imagine how her father must feel. But if the look on his face was any measure, he was beyond devastated.

Her uncle Sam sat quietly in a chair near the door taking in the whole scene without comment.

How would her mom handle this shocking news flash? Alex gasped and then covered her mouth. She needed to call her mom.

Charlie's fists clenched and flexed as he paced before his parents. "And what do you think now, Mother? Did I fall in love and marry someone else? No." He answered his own question with one growled word. "Did I become a lawyer and live in a big fancy house? No. I became a nature guide and live in a cabin in the woods. Have I been happy living all alone?" He stalked closer to his mother, who was now softly crying into her hands. "No. I've missed out on a life with the only woman I've ever loved. And…" His voice was choked with tears, and he turned to look at Alex. "I've missed out on my daughter's whole life. I never got to hold my baby."

Alex's chest physically hurt with the overwhelming rush of sympathy for the man who looked at her with so much pain. And love.

Audrey lifted her glasses and wiped her eyes. "Even if Kate thought you were dead, how could she keep our grandchild from us? If she had told us, it all could've been cleared up, and you could've had your life together."

Her grandmother's question set off a spike of anger. Alex pushed away from the wall and found her voice. "Don't you dare blame this on my mom. And I can tell you exactly why she kept the knowledge of me from you." She wiped away tears and cleared her throat. "You told her the love of her life was dead, and you never called back to tell her he'd returned. You kept life-altering news from her on purpose for your own selfish reasons. She was heartbroken and about to become a twenty-year-old single mother. She knew you didn't like her and was afraid you'd try to take me away from her."

"I'm sorry," Audrey said and reached a hand toward Alex. "I'm so very sorry. I thought I was doing the right thing. I—"

"Enough!" Charlie roared, seeming to come out of his moment of silence. "I can't talk to you right now. I can't listen to your excuses and empty apologies. We're leaving." He guided Alex from the room and out to the backyard.

Luke left his spot beside Dawn, took both of her hands and studied her face. "What happened? Are you all right?"

"I will be. Can we get Cody and go home? And can Charlie come over?"

"Of course. Cody, we need to go, buddy," he called to his nephew.

"I'll follow you over to your house," her father said.

"I'll ride with my... With Charlie." She could see the concern on Luke's face and loved that he was worried about her. "I'll be okay." After giving his hands a squeeze, she let go and they followed Charlie around the side of the house.

Once she was in her father's Jeep, she took what felt like the first deep breath since she'd first seen him standing by the barbecue grill, but she had no idea what to say or where to begin. It was quiet. Too quiet. Not even the radio was on. Only the rumble of the Jeep—and too many lost years—filled the space around them.

"I'm sorry about all of this," Charlie said. "So very, very sorry."

"You don't need to apologize for anything. You're a victim in this whole mess. Just like me and my mom."

"So all this time your mother truly thought I was dead?"

"Yes. She thought you were gone before she even realized she was pregnant. When she found out I was on the way…" A hot, prickly knot formed in her throat, and she swallowed hard against it. "She said it was like a miracle that God had given her a piece of you."

Charlie wiped his eyes and let out a long, slow exhale. "You know something weird? After my accident I was on a lot of heavy painkillers and I had these crazy fever dreams, and the most common one was of Katie with a baby. When I got home from Belize, I couldn't believe she'd married someone else. It just didn't make any sense. I called the only phone number I had, and her roommate said she'd moved out and didn't leave any forwarding information. I was shocked, and thought she really was avoiding me. I was still healing physically, but after that news, the thing that hurt most wasn't my leg and head." He absently rubbed the faded scar on his face. "It was my heart. I had a lot of emotional healing to do."

"It's because she was afraid your parents would find her and try to take me away. She knew your dad had lots of high-profile connections." Alex was glad they were driving. Somehow, it seemed easier to talk while they weren't staring at one another, searching for lost moments.

"My poor, sweet Katie girl. That breaks my heart all over again. I almost went to New York to search for her on several occasions, but—" He pounded his fist against the steering wheel. "Why did I let anything stop me from going to find her? I should've done everything in my power to track her down. If only I had, this whole horrible mess would've been cleared up."

"You can't think in what-ifs. Mom is going to do the same thing. She'll say, if only she'd been brave enough to tell them she was pregnant. If only she hadn't hidden herself away."

He chuckled. "How'd you get so smart?"

The sound of his laugh startled her because it sounded like a male version of her own. She adjusted the shoulder strap of her seat belt and shifted in her seat to get a better look at him. He rubbed a hand through his short blond beard, reminding her of a thoughtful Viking.

"Wait," he said. "I know the answer to my question. You take after your mother. She always amazed me with her brilliance."

"She's a doctor and has a family practice with three others."

He shot her a big smile. "I'm not surprised."

"It's a cruel twist of fate, and we've all been hurt by this, but the way I see it, none of it is your fault."

"Oh, really? How do you figure that?"

"Well, I estimate at least ninety-eight percent of it rests squarely with…someone else."

He pulled up behind Luke at a stop sign. "My manipulative mother. I'm sorry that this was your introduction to your grandmother."

"I actually met her briefly at the Acorn Café a few days ago, and she was very nice to me. So at least I have a good memory of our very first meeting."

He snorted. "I don't know how I can ever forgive my mother, or myself for not going to New York and searching until I found Kate. This whole nightmare of a disaster could've been prevented, and it feels like I'm being punished for something. I could've spent all these years with the two of you. And not alone. I wouldn't have missed your whole life."

"I guess we have a lot to catch up on. So you've never married, either?"

"No. I never could trust anyone enough after that. I've both loved and hated Kate all these years. All because of my own mother's lies."

The way his jaw was clenching, she was surprised she didn't hear his teeth cracking. "She still loves you. She never stopped. Do you want to see her or talk to her?"

"Oh, my God. Of course! I want to see her right now. I want to hold her and ask her if there's a chance that she'll ever forgive me."

"She's going to be shocked and thrilled beyond belief." Alex looked at his strong, handsome profile and tried to imagine what her mom would think when she saw him. "She's going to be over-the-moon happy."

He smiled and reached across the console to pat her arm. "I know the feeling."

"How should we tell her? Over the phone? In person?"

"You've had so much more time with your mom and know her best. What do you think?"

"I would really like to see her face when she finds out. When she sees you. And if we call her and she finds out when she's all alone, she'll make herself crazy. I'll call and tell her I need her to come to Oak Hollow right away."

"And you're sure she'll come? Because I can get on a plane today if I need to. I'll drive to the airport this second with only the clothes on my back."

His eagerness made Alex teary-eyed. Thank goodness he hadn't moved on. If she'd come here and discovered him married, it would've made for a very tricky situation. "She'll come. I'm sorry to make you wait, but I think an in-person reunion will be so awesome."

He rubbed his beard thoughtfully and then smiled. "I know the perfect place for a reunion. If you can get her here, I'll set everything up."

"It's a deal."

"Now, tell me all about yourself and your mother and everything I've missed," he said and drove past the cemetery where he was thankfully *not* buried.

"My name is Alexandra Charlotte. It was her female play on the name Charles Alexander."

"I love it. I don't suppose you have my last name?"

"No, but only because she wanted to keep me safe."

Chapter Thirteen

Luke glanced in his rearview mirror but couldn't see Alexandra's face because of the setting sun glinting off the windshield of Charlie's Jeep.

"Uncle Luke, Charlie is her daddy?"

"That's right." Unfortunately, the kids had overheard some of the adults' conversation, and he was trying his best to explain to a child who had a hundred questions what was happening with Alexandra. He had plenty of his own and hated that she'd been blindsided by this. If only he'd realized she believed Charlie was dead, he would've told her and set up a more private meeting between them.

His mind drifted back to the unhealthy thought that she might stay in Texas longer now that she'd discovered her father was alive. He wanted more time with her, but also feared it, because he was rapidly growing more attached. More time together might lead to him and his nephew becoming *too* attached and dependent on her in their daily lives.

"Cody, I need you to remember that Alexandra is only visiting Oak Hollow, and she'll be leaving in several weeks. She will get back onto an airplane and fly far away to New York City."

"New York City?"

"That's right." He turned onto Cherry Tree Lane. "She has to go home, but since she has family here, maybe she'll come back to visit another time."

"Is New York City on my map?"

"It sure is. I'll show you when we get home. We can add a pushpin and mark it as one of the places you want to go."

"Okay. Put a pushpin. A red one."

"You got it, buddy."

They could visit her, but what kind of relationship could they have with her an airplane flight away? He didn't want a long-distance arrangement. And that certainly wasn't what Cody needed. His nephew needed daily structure and stability. He needed a mother figure in his life.

Luke pulled into his driveway and rubbed a jaw that ached from clenching. "We're home, kiddo. Looks like it will be sandwiches for supper tonight."

"Peanut butter and jelly?"

"Sounds like a plan."

* * *

With her dad sitting in a chair across from her, Alex settled on Luke's blue sofa, dialed her mom's number and switched it to speakerphone.

"Hi, honey. Are you already back from your dinner?"

Charlie pressed a fist against his mouth and closed his eyes as soon as he heard Kate's voice.

"Yes. It was…very informative," Alex said.

"What's wrong? I can hear it in your voice."

She glanced at her dad, and he smiled and nodded encouragement. "It was a very emotional day, but I learned a lot. Mom, I need you to come to Oak Hollow. Please." She continued before her mother had time to argue or decline. "You said you'd come if I really needed you, and I do. Will you come tomorrow? Or tonight?"

"Tonight? Alexandra Charlotte, what happened?"

"I can explain it all better to you in person. There are things I want to show you. Things I want to share with you. Good things, Mom. Please, say you'll come as soon as you can."

"Okay, honey. I'm not sure I can get packed and on a flight by tonight, and I need to make arrangements for one of the other doctors to take my appointments, but I'll try to fly out as soon as I can tomorrow."

"That would be great. Call me with your flight details, and I'll pick you up."

Her mom's fluttery laughter drifted over the phone. "How are you going to pick me up? Please tell me you didn't rent a car and are planning on driving."

The shock in her mom's voice was a touch insulting. She glanced at Charlie's half grin and felt her face warming. And with very unperfect timing, Luke walked into the living room and put plates of sandwiches on the coffee table. "No. I didn't rent a car."

"And no offense, honey, but you haven't driven in years. Not since you drove Uncle Leo's car and—"

"Mom!" Alex said, cutting her off before she finished the story about her running her uncle's car into a taxicab. "I have it covered. I'll be there to pick you up. Just let me know your itinerary as soon as you have it."

"And you promise you're all right?"

"Yes. I promise. I love you."

"Love you, too, honey. I'll start making arrangements and call you soon."

Alex hung up and flopped back against the couch cushion. "This is going to be so amazing."

"She sounds just the same," Charlie said, a dreamy expression on his face. He sat forward in his chair and braced his elbows on his knees. "Do you have any pictures of your mother?"

"I do." She opened the photos on her phone and handed it to Charlie. "This is a recent one I took of her at work. Just scroll through and you'll see snippets of our lives in Manhattan. When she calls back with flight information, I'll ask her to bring some of my baby pictures and other old photos."

"That would be wonderful. I've missed so much and can't wait to catch up on everything."

Luke sat beside her and draped an arm over the back of the couch. "It sounds like somebody needs some driving lessons. I know your license is still valid."

She shifted to face him and narrowed her eyes. "How do you know?"

Luke grinned. "Because I checked you out the day you showed up on my doorstep."

Charlie glanced up from the screen of her phone. "I'll teach her to drive. It's my fatherly duty." His trembling smile was a mixture of pride and pain.

"I know *how* to drive. I just haven't done it in a while." Alex winced at the thought of driving Luke's giant double-cab truck or Charlie's rugged Jeep with the big tires. "I depend on the subway, buses, taxis and my own two feet to get around Manhattan."

Her father chuckled. "I have the perfect car for you to practice in. It's a little 1969 convertible sports car that I had when I met your mother. I've kept it all this time because I never could bear to part with it. It's the one we drove around the summer she was here. It will be perfect for you to get some practice on the backroads."

"In that case, I'd appreciate the practice."

"How did you ever get a driver's license to begin with?" Luke asked.

"My great uncle, who lives out on Long Island, taught me. A few months after I got my license, I kind of banged up his car and haven't driven since. But in my defense, some of the New York City taxi drivers need a few safety lessons of their own." In an effort to change the cringeworthy topic of conversation, she motioned to the sandwiches he'd put on the coffee table. "I see you've made us something to eat."

"Since we didn't get to eat earlier, I thought y'all might be hungry. Cody and I already ate. He's had a bath and is playing in his room."

"Luke, I don't know yet when she'll arrive, but do you think there is any possibility you can drive me to the airport?"

"I'll work it out. Shouldn't be a problem."

"If he can't, I'll drive, and we will just have to have the reunion at the airport." Charlie turned the phone toward them, displaying a picture of her mother in a fancy black dress. "She looks just the same. So beautiful."

"That was a New Year's Eve party at our apartment."

"Is she dating anyone?"

"No, and she hasn't in a long time. And even when she did, it never got serious." In the last few years, she'd encouraged her mom to put more effort into dating, but now she was glad her mother hadn't listened.

Charlie's mouth curved up in a half smile and his fingers drummed in double time against his leg. "Do you think your mother will be open to the idea of me going to New York? I'd like to see what your life has been like."

Suddenly light-headed, she inhaled deeply, reminding herself to breathe. Having a father who wanted to make them a family of three was so surreal. "I imagine she'll like that." She leaned away from Luke and narrowed her eyes at him. "Wait a minute. Why in the hell didn't you tell me my father was alive?"

Luke's eyes widened and he tugged on one of her curls. "Because, I had no idea you thought he was dead. You never said anything about that part."

"I didn't?"

"Nope. And if you'll recall, you've been very secretive, and I just barely found out why you really came to Texas."

"Music time, Alexandra," Cody called out as he came into the room carrying her guitar and wearing Black Panther pajamas.

"You play the guitar?" Charlie asked with a big grin on his face.

"I do. And I write songs."

"And sings me to sleep like Mary Poppins," Cody added as he bounced from foot to foot.

Charlie chuckled. "I'd like to hear that."

Feeling suddenly shy, a blush warmed her face.

"At least I know there's something you get from me," her father said. "I'm also a musician and have my own band."

"Really? Mom never mentioned that."

"I didn't start playing until…after."

Cody thrust the guitar into her hands. "Music, please. Bedtime."

"It's a little early for bedtime, but we can play some songs," she said.

"I'm tired. Bedtime."

"Well, then, I guess we better get you tucked in, sugar boy."

"Sugar boy?" Cody giggled and repeated the nickname three times.

The lovely sound of his childish laughter added extra joy to her heart. "Since you like to put a spoonful of sugar in every recipe, I think it's a fitting name for you."

Everyone followed Cody into his superhero bedroom. He ran over to the map of the United States hanging on his wall. "New York City," the little boy said, and pointed to the red pushpin they'd added to mark the spot.

"Do you think you might want to come visit me?"

"Yes. I will visit."

Her dad leaned against the door frame while she helped Luke and Cody go through the child's regular bedtime routine. Stuffed animals arranged along the wall from tallest to shortest. Overhead light off. Night-light on. And, finally, a quick peek under the bed before the covers were pulled back. Once he was tucked in, she began to strum her guitar.

Charlie joined in on the Creedence Clearwater Revival song "Have You Ever Seen The Rain." The instant harmony of their voices surprised her. Alex had to let him take over at one point when emotion tightened her throat too much to sing. Her mom was going to cry like a baby when she heard the two of them singing together.

Cody fell asleep after six songs, and they tiptoed out of his bedroom. Luke excused himself to take a shower, and she suspected he was giving them more time to get to know one another. They used the opportunity to chat about everything from her first day of school to their favorite foods. For some reason it made her extra giddy that he shared her belief that ginger tastes like soap and liked to put cayenne pepper in his coffee.

Kate called with her next day's flight information. Everything was moving at a rapid pace, and they only had a matter of hours to wait.

"I better get going so I have time to clean my cabin before either of you sees it," Charlie said. "Let me know when you're ready to start those driving lessons."

"Can we please call it driving *practice*?"

He pressed his lips together, trying not to laugh. "Sure thing."

There was an awkward moment of not knowing what to do, so Alex stepped forward and hugged him. Even though they'd only known one another for a few hours, she already felt a connection to the man who was responsible for her existence.

He squeezed her extra tight as if making up for lost time, then stepped back and smiled. "This is one of the best days of my life."

"Mine, too. It's been so amazing. I'll see you tomorrow, and it will only get better."

He ducked his head as if trying to hide the tears in his eyes. "Good night."

"Try to get some sleep." She closed the front door behind him and propped her forehead against the smooth wood.

Please tell me I'm not going to wake up and realize this is a dream.

"Are you okay?" Luke asked from behind her.

"I'm really good." She turned as he put a CD into the stereo. His wet hair was in perfect disarray, running shorts showed off athletic legs and a T-shirt hugged every tempting dip and plane of his muscled torso. The slow beat of a country song changed the mood of the room, and her inner sex goddess stood up and growled.

"Come over here and let me hold you, sweetheart."

She stepped into his open arms and encircled his neck. He smelled of Irish Spring and spicy shaving cream. This man possessed a sexiness that went deeper than his outward appearance. And her heart was in danger of falling in love.

Luke cradled her head against his chest and could tell she was both exhausted and filled with excited energy. "Have you heard back from your mom?"

"Yes. She got a flight for tomorrow and will arrive at four thirty in the afternoon."

"I have to work in the morning but already talked to Anson about getting my afternoon covered. I'll swing by the house in time to get you, and Cody can stay with Hannah."

"Thank you for sticking around through all this craziness. A lot of guys wouldn't have." She trailed her fingers into his hair, making him shiver.

"Family is important. I get that." He wanted one of his own, and for a moment, he closed his eyes and held her tighter, letting himself pretend he could start one with her. Then he gave himself a mental slap. That dangerous thought was better left alone. He loosened his hold and eased away from her before crossing the room to check the front-door lock. "Why don't you go take a bath and relax."

Her eyebrows drew together, and her hand hovered momentarily in the air as if she wanted to touch him, but she let it drop to her side. "Okay. Got any bubble bath?"

"Um, no."

"You should see your expression." She shook her head. "They don't take your man card away if you do. There's a child in the house, and you could always blame it on him."

"This just gives you something else to shop for."

"True. I think I'll take a bath, anyway. I wish you could join me."

"Me, too. I bet you have one of those big soaker tubs."

"Are you kidding? In a New York apartment? My bathroom is smaller than yours."

He watched her walk away and really wanted to follow, especially when she glanced over her shoulder with a saucy grin that made his body come alive.

To keep himself busy, he checked emails and cleaned the kitchen. He was so deep in thoughts of what he'd like to do with her in private that she startled him when she slipped up from behind and wrapped her arms around his waist.

"I just wanted to thank you again for being here for me."

He turned in her embrace and tipped up her chin. "You know the kind of thank-you I like."

"I sure do." She raised onto her toes and kissed him like a woman starving.

To hell with being cautious. I only have a limited amount of time with her.

He lifted her to wrap her legs around his waist and filled his hands with her curves. "I want to take you to bed."

"What about Cody?"

He kissed the curve of her neck. "I figure parents do it all the time with children in the house. I just can't stay in bed with you all night this time, and you can't be as loud as you were when we had the place to ourselves," he said and grinned.

"Hey, I wasn't that loud."

He spun around, set her on the counter and slid his hand up the inside of her thigh to cup her heat, laughing when she gasped and moaned loudly. "Whatever you say, sweetheart."

They walked down the hallway, peeked into Cody's room to make sure he was sleeping and then continued to his bedroom, where he closed and locked the door.

Chapter Fourteen

Alex fidgeted, bouncing her knee and drumming her fingers against her thigh while Luke took the exit for the San Antonio airport. Charlie waited just as impatiently back in Oak Hollow. He'd texted with instructions several times. They'd take her mother out to the plot of land where Charlie had built a two-bedroom log cabin in the same spot where he and her mother had camped together twenty-five years ago.

Wonder if that's where I was conceived?

"Sweetheart, you're rattling the whole truck with your nerves over there." Luke stopped at a traffic light and tucked her hair behind her ear, his fingers lingering on her skin. "What has you so worried?"

The tenderness of his touch felt good, and she

clasped his hand to her cheek until he needed to put it back onto the steering wheel. "It's not so much worry as it is excitement. I hope my mom's flight isn't late."

"Weather's good, so I bet it's on time. Do you want me to come inside with you or wait in the cell-phone lot?"

"I think maybe you should come inside. If I'm alone with her, she'll ask too many questions, and I might give away the surprise. If you don't mind parking, I could use the support."

"You got it." He pulled into short-term parking and they had to drive around for a bit to find a spot big enough for his truck.

Inside the airport, Alex and Luke stood near the bottom of the escalator where her mom would come down to the baggage-claim area. She fidgeted and ran the toe of her shoe across a crack in the tile. "How am I going to resist telling her about my dad until we get back to Oak Hollow?"

"I'll help you keep the conversation veered in other directions, so you don't spill the beans." He put an arm around her shoulders, tipped up her chin and kissed her.

"Thank you, Officer Walker. You're a good public servant. There might be more rewards coming your way."

"I'm counting on it."

Tingles rippled across her skin, his steamy gaze calling up memories of their lovemaking. Before she had time to form a response, she saw her mom's favorite burgundy leather wedge sandals step onto the top of the escalator, followed by her long legs in slim, dark jeans and an emerald-green wrap top. She'd always found her mom to be the most elegant woman she knew. Alex couldn't keep the enormous smile off her face and waved eagerly while waiting for the moving stairs to bring her mother to ground level. She was so excited to share her amazing, life-changing discovery, and couldn't wait to see her face when she saw Charlie.

They embraced and then Kate held her daughter's cheeks and studied her face. "You look happy. Really happy. I was worried you were holding back on the phone and would dissolve into tears when I got here."

"Nope. I'm truly good. There are just things I want to share with you."

"What is it you're so excited to share with me that you couldn't tell me over the phone?" Kate asked.

"It's something that has to wait until we get to Oak Hollow."

"Alexandra Charlotte Roth, why are you being so mysterious?"

A man looking at his phone bumped into them, mumbled an apology and kept walking.

"You'll just have to trust me." She linked their arms and guided her a few steps to the side, where Luke was standing. "I'd like you to meet Officer Luke Walker of the Oak Hollow Police Department. Also known as my temporary landlord."

Kate took his offered hand. "So nice to meet you."

"It's a pleasure to meet you, too, Dr. Roth."

"Please, call me Kate."

"Let's get your suitcase and get out to Luke's truck," Alex said.

"Oh, good. I was worried you'd driven after all."

"No, but…" She coughed and bit the inside of her cheek. "I have someone who's offered to help me practice that skill." She'd almost said that it was her *father*.

How am I going to stand keeping this secret until we get back to Oak Hollow?

Luke caught her wide-eyed glance and grinned. "I figured it would be a lot less stressful for her to practice driving out in the country."

"Good idea," Kate said. "There are a lot less wild taxi drivers to run into on a country road."

"Very funny, Mom."

While they waited for the luggage carousel from her flight to start spinning, Kate grabbed her daughter's hand. "Luke, will you watch for a hard-shell suitcase covered with conversation hearts while Alex and I get a drink?"

"Sure. No problem."

She had no choice but to follow when her mom pulled her along toward the coffee cart set up near the exit.

"Your Luke is really cute."

"He's not *my* Luke. He's just my temporary landlord." She said the words but couldn't hide her grin and flushed cheeks.

"I get the feeling there's more between the two of you than a landlord-and-tenant relationship. I can't help but notice a particular grin on your face. I've seen it before. Is he the reason you wanted me to come to Texas?"

Alex wouldn't go into too much detail, but she loved that she could talk to her mother about love and romance. She debated if she should use Luke as an excuse, but she didn't want to give her mom a false impression. "No, he's not the reason."

"I fell in love with your father the day I met him. Sometimes it happens fast, and you just know it's right."

"There's definitely a mutual attraction between us. We've agreed to have fun while I'm here, but nothing serious because I'm only here for a little while. And New York is too far away for a real relationship."

"Does Luke know the whole story about your father?"

"Yes." Her heart rate picked up speed. "He could tell something was up and I told him before we went over to my grandparents' house. Being a police officer, he has good instincts."

"Do any of the Hargroves know who you are yet?" Kate asked as she paid for three bottles of water.

"Yes, they do." She blew out a slow breath. "I intended to wait as you suggested, but apparently, our resemblance is striking enough that it didn't take them long to start asking questions and figure things out. My uncle Sam is married to a woman named Dawn. They have a son and a daughter, Timothy and Mary." She rushed her mom along before she had a chance to ask more questions. "It looks like he found your bag."

Luke was leaning against a post looking uncomfortable with Kate's heart-covered luggage. She took her mother's very feminine bag and handed him a bottle of water. They headed for the exit, weaving around other travelers on their way to the parking garage.

"I really appreciate you driving Alex here to get me."

"Happy to do it, ma'am."

"Alex, I have some good news. I saw Dr. Carrington, and he told me the job is down to you and one other candidate. It's not a for-sure thing yet, but he hinted strongly that they're leaning toward offering you the position."

"Really? That's amazing." A thrill zinged through her. "I thought they'd want someone with way more experience than I have."

"I told you they would love you once they met you."

"This is the job you've hoped for?" Luke asked as they stepped onto the garage elevator.

"Yes." Something in his tone dampened her enthusiasm.

"I'm so proud of my daughter. It's a very sought-after music-therapy position at a clinic in the same building where I have my medical practice. Openings come up very rarely."

"That's wonderful," he said.

Alex wasn't convinced he was happy about her possible job in Manhattan. His smile didn't reach his eyes and there were creases between his eyebrows.

Could he possibly be hoping I'll stay, or am I subconsciously projecting my starry-eyed fantasies onto him?

As hard as she tried to resist, she was falling for this handsome cowboy, and leaving Oak Hollow was going to be so much harder than she ever could've imagined.

On the drive, Luke made sure to ask lots of questions about New York and, like a tour guide, told Kate about everything they were passing. Alex knew he was doing it to keep her from blowing the secret, and she was extremely grateful.

"See that hill in the distance with the flat top?" Kate said. "That's one of the spots where Charlie and I camped. It was so hot that we sat in the river to cool off in the middle of the night. There were so many stars. I've been looking forward to seeing a sky full of stars like that again on this trip."

"In that case, I know the perfect place to drive you," Luke said, and shot Alex a knowing grin.

Night had fallen as they neared the spot where they'd meet Charlie. It was near his cabin, and a location that held special meaning. Alex kept her mom busy looking at photos on her cell phone, and she hadn't noticed their last few turns.

Kate glanced up when Luke parked near a bluff that looked out over the river and hills beyond. "Why are we…here?" She sucked in a sharp breath. "Alex, how do you know this spot? Is my Charlie buried here?"

"No, he's not buried here." Her mother's bewildered heartache was as strong as the trembling of her hand. "Let's get out, and I'll show you."

Seconds after they climbed out of the truck, Charlie stepped out from behind a large tree. "Katie. My beautiful Katie." His voice was a husky whisper. A heart-wrenching plea. He reached out, arms open wide, inviting her to come closer. Inviting her to return to his life.

"Charlie?" She clasped a hand to her chest and stumbled back against her daughter. "Is it you? How? How is it you?"

"It's me, princess." He stepped forward tentatively. "It's me."

"Mom, go to him." Alex urged her mother toward the love of her life.

"Charlie." Kate ran forward and they fell into a tender embrace filled with enough emotion to bring tears to anyone's eyes.

Alex settled into Luke's arms and rested her cheek against his heart, the steady beat like music to her ears. "I'm afraid this is a dream I'll wake from."

"It's real, sweetheart. You were brave enough

to come here and search for your roots. Your parents are finally together because of you. Look how happy they are."

Her father held her mother so fiercely, so tenderly, with her head tucked under his chin. "I've missed you every single day," Charlie said. "I've never stopped loving you."

Kate clasped his face with both hands and stared up at him, but then her brow furrowed. "Why did you let me believe you were dead? I don't understand." She dropped her hands and pushed away. "How could you do that to me?"

Alex sucked in a breath and squeezed Luke's arm. Her mother's confusion and anger were obvious. This beautiful reunion couldn't fall apart now.

"Kate, it's not like that." Charlie reached for her again, but she took another step back. "It was all a horrible misunderstanding. I thought you had married someone else."

"What?" She glanced at Alex and Luke, blinking rapidly as if she could clear the confusion.

"Mom, listen to him. He's telling the truth. It was all his mother's doing."

"It's true," Luke confirmed.

Kate turned back to Charlie and accepted his outstretched hand, clasping it to her heart. "Your mother did this to us?" Her tone conveyed her shock.

"Unfortunately, yes. I only learned the truth yesterday." He smiled at Alex. "And met my beautiful, talented daughter." His voice caught on the last word.

Alex left the comfort of Luke's arms and shared her first family hug with both of her parents. Her heart was so full it threatened to pound from her chest. When she smiled over her shoulder at Luke, he pulled his phone from his pocket.

"Everyone look this way," Luke called to them. "Smile so I can get your first family picture."

Once the hugging and crying and photo taking was done, they walked to Charlie's cabin, which turned out to be a gorgeously crafted masterpiece with a tree-of-life carved onto the front door. Her tattoo suddenly took on more meaning, almost as if it was a family symbol she'd sensed in her blood.

After making plans to meet up at Luke's house the next morning and go to the Fourth of July celebration, they left her parents to get reacquainted and find their way back to one another. As they drove away from Charlie's cabin, Luke called Anson and discovered Cody and Hannah were sleeping, and it was best to leave him at their house for the night.

"I have a family," Alex said when he ended the phone call. "After so many years of it just being me and my mom, I have all these new family members to get to know. A father. An aunt, uncle and cousins. Grandparents." With a sigh, she rubbed her temples. Alex had witnessed her mom's capacity for forgiveness, but Audrey Hargrove would likely have to do a ton of groveling and explaining before she was granted absolution. "Even though we'll have to wait and see how the relationship with my grandmother works out. Oh, Luke, I'm sorry."

He shot her a narrow-eyed glance. "For what?"

"For going on and on about family when you've lost so much." She stretched across the center console and kissed his cheek.

"There's no need to apologize. I'm happy for you."

"Cody is a lucky little boy to have you in his life. Do you want to have more children?" The second the question was out of her mouth, she held her breath, worried he'd think she was hinting at a future family together.

Is that what I want? A future with Luke?

"Sure. I'd love to give him siblings." He glanced her direction and smiled. "Are you hungry? We can stop for something before we get home."

Home.

A flutter filled her belly. That one simple word held so much meaning and possibility. "I am hungry, now that you mention it. Let's get takeout. I don't want to be around a lot of people right now. I just want to chill with you."

"Works for me." His hand slid into hers, thumb stroking the center of her palm.

Once they were home with a bag of tacos, they ate and talked about the highlights of the day. Now that he no longer needlessly aggravated her on purpose, Luke was easy to talk to. He actually listened, not just murmuring occasional indistinct sounds to give the impression of interest, like her last boy-friend. And it didn't hurt that Luke looked really hot in his cowboy attire while listening. She studied his kind, chocolate-drop eyes and let contentment settle over her, ready to soak up the pleasure of his company while she still had the chance.

"Are you tired?" she asked.

"No." His heated gaze stroked her as if it was a physical touch. "I want to get you naked."

She stood, untied her wrap dress and let it fall to the floor, revealing her pink bra-and-panty set. "I'm going to take a shower." With her hands running through her hair, she stepped back and gave him what she hoped was a sexy smile. "Care to join me?"

He was off the couch in a split second, untucking his own shirt and chasing her across the room as she laughed and ran down the hallway.

Chapter Fifteen

Saturday morning, Luke answered a knock on the front door. "Morning, Anson. Thanks for bringing this kiddo home and for keeping him last night." He ruffled his nephew's hair as he ran past calling out for Alexandra.

"Happy to do it." Anson motioned for him to come outside.

He followed his friend onto the front porch and closed the door. "What's up? Do you need me to work today after all?"

"No, it's covered. I'm headed to the station now."

"I really appreciate not having to work today. It'll be good to spend the time with Cody doing something fun."

"You need to thank my wife for that. She's stuck on the idea of you and Alexandra being together."

Luke pinched the bridge of his nose, wishing it was that simple. "If she was staying in the same state it might be possible, but she's not. Besides, we have an agreement to have fun while she's here, but that's all."

"And then it just ends?"

"That's the idea." Luke sat on the swing and rubbed his hands roughly through his hair. "In such a short time she's slipped into our lives and…I don't know, just fits." He studied the huge grin on Anson's face. "You know what I'm going through, don't you?"

"Yup. This is strangely similar to what happened with me and Tess. She came to town to do a job with no intention of staying. And then she discovered what she thought she wanted wasn't that important, and what she really wanted was me. I'm irresistible." They both laughed.

He really didn't need his friend giving him false hope. "I don't think the same will be true for our situation. Apparently, there's a prestigious job that she'll probably get. Plus, Charlie is thinking about moving to Manhattan. She'll want to be there to get to know him."

"Wow," Anson said and sat in one of the rocking chairs. "It's hard to imagine Charlie in New York City. When you called and told me about Alexandra being his daughter, I couldn't believe it."

"It's like something out of a movie. Not what you think will happen in your own little town."

"Cody said something about Alexandra staying to be his nanny. He called her Mary Poppins."

"Damn. I keep talking to him about her leaving, but I'm worried he doesn't really understand. Everything always works out in the movies he watches."

And life was not a movie.

When Alex's parents arrived at Luke's house, they were holding hands and smiling like two teenagers in love for the first time. And since they were each other's first and only loves, it was fitting. Seeing her mother this happy was an amazing thing that almost brought her romantic heart to tears every time she thought about it.

"You look lovely," her mom said. "Is that a new dress?"

"Yes, it is." Alex twirled in her blue-and-white polka-dot dress, the full skirt rippling around her. "I bought it at a wonderful vintage clothing shop on the square. We definitely have to go shopping there. You'll love it."

Luke chuckled.

Alex pointed at him. "You hush."

"What?" His grin spread wider. "I didn't say a thing."

"But I saw you thinking it. You were about to say something about me always coming home with shopping bags."

"If the shoe fits…" He left the statement hanging.

"Oh, I need new shoes," Kate said.

Luke and Charlie shared a conspiratorial look and shook their heads.

"Alexandra," her father said. "Bring your guitar to the picnic today. I want you to join my band on stage for a song or two."

Excitement and nerves fluttered in her chest. "Really? I've never performed in front of a big crowd on a stage. What if I don't know any of the songs your band plays?"

"I was thinking of the first one you played for Cody on Thursday night would be a good choice. The Creedence Clearwater Revival song." Charlie gazed at Kate and his smile widened. "We used to listen to that album together."

"Mom, is that why you've always played that album?"

"It sure is."

"And I know there are a few other songs you'll know," Charlie added. "We play a lot of the classic rock you seem to favor."

Kate wrapped an arm around her daughter and kissed her cheek. "I would love to hear the two of you play together. Please, do it."

"I'll get it." Cody ran out of the room and returned quickly with her guitar case, then thrust it into her hands. "You play music with your daddy."

"Well, I sure can't deny a request from my biggest fan."

Since Charlie had musical equipment in his Jeep,

he drove, but the rest of them walked to the town square for the big celebration.

"Aren't they the cutest?" Kate whispered to her daughter as they walked behind Luke and Cody.

"Totally. Like two peas in a pod. I did a painting of them walking down the sidewalk just like they are now."

Luke glanced over his shoulder and smiled, making butterflies dance in her belly.

Her mother linked an arm through hers. "I decided to take a short leave of absence from work so I can spend more time here with your father. I'll fly back to New York with you at the end of the month. Since Charlie is talking about moving to Manhattan, I told him he could live with us. I hope that's okay with you?"

"Of course. I don't want the two of you to miss another second of being together." Her mother's beaming smile was all the confirmation she needed that it was the right answer. "Do you think we will get together to talk with his parents about all this before we go home?"

"Neither of us are very excited about talking to her, but I think it will have to be done. Especially if he's going to move to Manhattan."

The town square was a sea of red, white and blue, with rows of tents selling food and crafts, and music floating from the gazebo over the crowd of happy people. They ate too much, and Alex ended up playing and singing three songs on stage with her father's band, The Nature Boys.

On the way back from getting snow cones with Cody, Alex watched the same woman from the hardware store hugging Luke again. She came up behind him, curious to hear what they were talking about.

"I found a house to rent until I can buy one," the woman said. "I'm so happy to finally be settling here. Maybe you can show me around sometime. I'd like to know where the best places are to go fishing."

"Sure. I love to fish," Luke said, and didn't seem bothered by her hand still on his arm.

Alex's stomach turned and then tightened into an uncomfortable knot. They were bonding over something they both liked to do. An activity she'd never even done. She took a deep breath and reminded herself she would be leaving and had no real claim on this man. She and Luke had an agreement… but that would end once she went home. And this woman was staying here in Oak Hollow. Who was she to keep them apart if they liked one another?

Alex wasn't going to alert him to her presence yet, still hoping to hear more of their conversation, even though it hurt, but Cody tugged on his uncle's arm.

"Uncle Luke, tiger blood flavor." He held up his red snow cone for inspection.

"Yum. Where's mine?" Luke turned, dislodging the other woman's arm, and smiled at Alex.

She thrust his snow cone forward, thankfully resisting her childish desire to drop it on the other woman's shoes. "Here you go."

"Alexandra, this is Gwen Clark. She's new to town and joining her uncle's medical practice. Dr. Clark has been Cody's doctor since he was born."

Alex felt better when his arms slid around her waist and he pulled her against his side.

"Alexandra is visiting from New York. She also has family here in town."

The two women shook hands and exchanged pleasantries. Gwen made an excuse to leave and hurried away through the crowd.

Luke took a bite of his snow cone and then kissed her cheek with cold lips. "Is that tension between your eyebrows because you're jealous?"

"Of what?" She tried to play dumb but knew he wasn't buying it. His grin was that of a ladies' man who knew how attractive he was. "Just eat your snow cone," she said, and pushed it against his smirking mouth.

They spent time with her uncle Sam's family, but her grandparents did not show up for the event, and no one mentioned them. The day was too nice, and she supposed no one wanted to mess it up with a discussion about family drama. That was better left for another day.

She found a moment to go into the vintage shop with her mom, Tess and Jenny, and was excited at how quickly she'd made new friends.

* * *

Late in the afternoon, Luke knew his parenting luck had run out. Something had upset Cody, and no one was exactly sure what it was. He sat on their picnic blanket rocking and clasping his noise-canceling headphones to his ears, refusing to listen to any of them.

Luke started picking up their belongings and the food they had spread out on the blanket. "I better take him home and get him calmed down. Hopefully we can come back later for the fireworks."

"Wait. Let me try something." Alexandra poured her water onto the ground, wiped out her plastic cup with a napkin and then held out a hand to Luke. "Can I borrow your pocketknife, please?"

Curious as to what she had in mind, he handed it over, and watched in surprise when she took off her long strand of red, white and blue beads and cut the cord. Glass beads clattered musically into her empty cup. She spread three napkins onto the picnic blanket in front of Cody, then put one different-colored glass sphere onto each napkin and finally held the jumble of colors in his line of vision.

Cody rocked a moment longer, but his gaze fastened on the mixed-up beads in the cup. He reached in, took a red one and put it on the napkin with the same color. Next, he picked up a blue one and stopped rocking.

Luke couldn't believe she had ruined her necklace just so Cody would have something to sort.

When she turned her head and smiled at him, his chest tightened with something that felt dangerously close to falling in love. He had the very strong urge to gather her into his arms and kiss her until she promised to stay, forever.

He settled for sitting beside her. "Thank you. I'll buy you a new necklace."

"I appreciate that, but there's no need. I can just restring it once we get home. Cody can even help me make it into a pattern. That might be something new he likes to do."

"You're one very clever lady."

After the evening fireworks show—that Cody thankfully tolerated well—one more band took the stage. Charlie and Kate had already said their goodbyes, eager to spend more time alone. Luke knew the feeling. He couldn't seem to get enough private time with Alexandra and wanted to soak up every moment possible before she left. Being with her was different than it had been with other women, and he couldn't put his finger on why. The sex was amazing, but it was more than just the physical. Being with her was easier. Comfortable.

Cody had fallen asleep curled up between them. He lifted the child into his arms, head resting on his shoulder, and kissed his forehead. He often took the opportunity for more cuddles when his nephew was asleep and not at risk of pushing away physical affection. "Alexandra, are you ready to get this little guy home?"

She wrapped her arms around both of them.

"First, can we have one more dance? I love this song."

"I'd love to." Luke kissed her lips softly and cradled her head against his free shoulder. He no longer cared who saw their public displays of affection. Let people talk. It's not like it was something new for him. His reputation had been in place for years.

With a sleeping child sandwiched between them, they danced to the mellow strains of a country love song under the starry night sky, three hearts beating together…like a family.

Chapter Sixteen

On Sunday morning, Luke found his nephew in front of the TV watching *The Sound of Music*. "Morning, kiddo." He ruffled his hair, and then followed his nose to the kitchen, where Alexandra was making pancakes and sausages. As he liked to do, he stood in the doorway and admired her elegant form moving about to her own rhythm. A rhythm that never failed to arouse him. And, dangerously, touch his heart.

She turned around with a plate and blew him a kiss. "Yes, I knew you were there the whole time."

"Oh, you did?"

"Why do you think I added extra wiggle to my dance?" She swayed her hips in an exaggerated side-to-side move, emphasizing her point, and then winked before turning. "Cody," she called out. "Your pancake is ready."

His nephew ran into the kitchen before Luke could do anything about his rising desire. She giggled, as if knowing good and well the state she'd put him in. Sexy little devil.

"Pancakes!" Cody yelled repeatedly and ran around the kitchen table.

"Sit down before it gets cold, sugar boy." She put his plate on the table. The pancake had strawberry eyes, a blueberry nose and a chocolate-chip mouth.

"Do I get a face on my breakfast, too?" Luke asked.

"Of course." She prepared two more plates and joined them at the table. "Any plans for today?"

"Flowers to my mommy," Cody said and pointed his fork at Alexandra. "And you go, too."

She shot a questioning glance at Luke, and he nodded. Cody wanted her there…and so did he. Libby would have liked her, and no doubt been on board with Tess about the matchmaking.

"I'd like that very much," she replied. "After our visit to the cemetery, what do you think about going out to Charlie's cabin?"

"I like Charlie. He helped me fish." Cody stuffed a bite of sausage into his mouth.

"I have to work tonight," Luke said, forgetting he hadn't already told her.

"I didn't realize that. I'm sorry we made so much noise this morning. You should still be sleeping."

She poured syrup on her pancake and passed the bottle.

"It's okay. I couldn't sleep. I don't have to go in until six tonight. I can catch a nap right before."

"I thought you didn't really have to work nights since…" Her eyes cut toward Cody, who was busy rearranging his chocolate chips into a crooked grin.

"I need to make up some hours for trading shifts and taking time off."

She put down the bite she'd been about to pop into her mouth. "Because you took off to drive me to the airport?"

"Totally worth it."

"I guess I owe you another reward."

The way she bit the corner of her lip never failed to spark desire. Luke took her hand under the table and stroked her palm with his thumb. Slow little circles then quick flicks across the center, imitating something he knew made her tremble with pleasure. "I like rewards."

She shivered right on cue, and her breathing rate increased. Exactly the effect he was going for. *That's right, sweetheart. Two can play this game.*

It was a cloudy day with a hint of coming rain in the air that had thankfully held off long enough for yesterday's Fourth of July picnic to be a huge success. They first walked to their neighbor's yard to cut a bouquet of summer flowers and then headed toward the cemetery.

Luke took Alexandra's hand, and when she shot

him a questioning glance and then cut her eyes toward Cody, he shrugged. "I know I said we'd keep the physical affection private, but he doesn't seem the least bit concerned about it."

At that moment, Cody turned around and looked at them while walking backward. "Where's your mommy?"

"She's at Charlie's cabin."

"Okay." He spun around and continued down the sidewalk.

"See." Luke lifted her hand to kiss her knuckles. "Doesn't bother him. And I figure that if he sees I care about you like he does, I'll have more credibility when it comes time to explain things after you go home. He'll know that I understand his feelings. I hope. Sharing the sorrow seemed to help after his mom died."

"I really didn't mean to come here and disrupt your lives."

"Grief was eating at both of us, and it's good for us to be reminded that we're still among the living and should take advantage of what's around us. We needed a bit of a shake-up in our lives." *We needed you.*

"In that case, I'm glad I could be of service. Think Ms. Poppins would be proud of me?"

"Yes, she would, sweetheart."

"So, you and Cody fish with my dad?"

"Sometimes. He also took us rafting."

"Will you teach me to fish?"

"Of course."

They entered through the cemetery gates. Cody placed the flowers in the center of his mother's grave, walked around it three times and then sat at the foot and arranged pebbles on the stone border.

Luke picked up a rock from Libby's headstone. "I wonder where this came from. It's pretty."

"I put it there," she said. "Remember when I asked you where the cemetery was?"

"Were you looking for your father's grave?"

"Yes. And I was so confused when I couldn't find it. It's so crazy the way things have turned out." She motioned to his parents' graves. "Tell me something about your mom and dad."

"They were great parents. Dad taught me to play ball, and Mom loved Christmas more than anyone I've ever known."

"I understand that. I'm kind of Christmas crazy. It's my favorite season."

"Then you'll love the way Oak Hollow does Christmas." The statement hung in the air between them. She wouldn't be here at Christmas time, and that made him sad. "Are you ready to go, buddy? You can play in the woods around Charlie's cabin." He stroked his nephew's dark hair and realized he needed to take him to the barbershop for a trim.

"Okay." Cody moved to his mother's headstone and leaned in to whisper, then pulled a pale pink stem of snapdragons from the bouquet he'd placed on her grave. Instead of heading for the front gate, he went straight to Alexandra and held out the flower.

"For me?" She kneeled in front of him and accepted the blossoms. "Thank you so much, sugar boy."

Cody shuffled his boots in the grass. "My mommy said you can share her flowers."

Luke's gut clenched, and he pressed his fingers to his eyes.

"I love this flower and will keep it forever." She kissed his forehead, and Cody didn't pull away.

Luke met her gaze and saw an emotion similar to his playing out in her expression. They were both too choked up to speak as they walked toward the front gate, especially when Cody squeezed in between them and took each of their hands, a very unusual move for him. And just like the night before, the three of them moved together.

Luke had to remind Cody that she was only here temporarily, just like the Mary Poppins in the movie. It might need to become a daily reminder, but he couldn't bear to bring it up and ruin this moment.

They'd have to make their way alone when she returned to her home and life in New York. It would once again be just the two of them, a struggling uncle and nephew. He'd been pushing aside this fact and needed to remind himself, as well. But they had both grown so attached to her in such a short time. It was going to be much harder than he'd anticipated.

One afternoon the following week, Alex was watering the flowers and herbs they'd planted while Cody picked dead petals off the blossoms.

"You know how I put the flower you gave me between two sheets of glass and hung it on the wall?"

"Like art. Because you love it?"

"That's right, and I always want to remember you giving it to me. If you'd like, I can help you do the same with the flowers you have pressed in the book. We'll need a much bigger frame. Then we can hang it on the wall."

"And remember my mommy forever?"

"Yes. Forever and ever." She turned off the water and watched a smile grow on his sweet little face.

"Okay." He hopped out of the flower bed and walked around her three times.

"Do you want to kick your new soccer ball around the yard?"

"It gets stuck," he said.

"What is it getting stuck on?"

"The grass. Too tall."

She wiggled her bare toes in the grass and then glanced at the lawn mower Luke had intended to use, until she'd distracted him with food and kisses. Something he'd said to her on their drive to the nursery—back before they were getting along— gave her an idea.

"Hey, sugar boy, do you know how to start this thing?"

"Pull, pull, pull." He jerked his arm back and then tapped the handle he referred to.

"Okay. Stand back while I get it started."

Cody giggled at her first try when her hand popped off the rubber handle. He outright laughed when her second attempt landed her on her bottom. But the third time was a success and he cheered, but then covered his ears and ran for the safety of the back porch.

She fiddled with a few levers and knobs and finally figured out how to make it go forward. With slow, steady passes, she mowed the grass into interesting designs. It wasn't like it couldn't be mowed over and erased, but she liked it even if it was temporary. When she'd first arrived, Luke would've had a fit about her doing this, but now, would he find it ridiculous or funny?

When Luke arrived home that evening, Cody met him at the door. "Come see, Uncle Luke. Come see, come see."

"Where are we going?"

"Art on the grass." Cody pulled him through the house.

He shot a wide-eyed glance over his shoulder at Alex. "Should I be worried?"

"You're the one who gave me the idea," she said and blew a kiss.

When he saw the artistic lawn maintenance, he laughed and put an arm around her waist.

The little boy jumped down onto the grass and ran through the designs like a racetrack while making car noises.

She rested her head on his shoulder and loved the warmth of his tall, strong body against her. And the big smile on his face as he watched his nephew play. "He's really coming out of his shell."

"Because of you, he's finally back to the kid I remember before we lost Libby."

The flutter in her chest brought tears to her eyes. Before she could form a reply, Cody ran back onto the deck.

"Uncle Luke, Alexandra made a plan."

"Oh, really? Do I even want to know what it is?"

"Probably not," she said, and couldn't hold back her giggle.

"I'll get it." Cody rushed into the house.

While the little boy was inside, she settled deeper into his embrace and couldn't wait to hear Luke's reaction to the outlandish plan they'd drawn up to turn the whole backyard into a fairy garden.

Chapter Seventeen

The days and nights went by with Luke and Alex each telling themselves that they could part as friends at the end of her trip and then go on with the rest of their lives. They grew closer despite warnings and reminders to themselves. They each spoke with Cody almost daily and mentioned something about her inevitable return to her home in Manhattan. In fact, they began to remind Cody that she was leaving so often that the little boy started saying it himself.

"I know. You'll go away like Mary Poppins," Cody would say and ask how many more days.

She helped Luke buy a secondhand piano and they rearranged the living-room furniture to make it fit. Cody was thrilled, practicing every day and singing like a little songbird. Alex had her own skill to practice and drove her dad's sports car around the winding country roads of the Texas Hill Country. Charlie also taught her to fish, and Luke and Cody laughed at her when she refused to put a worm on her hook.

Her parents rekindled their relationship and were as sappy as teenagers. They frequently got together with her uncle Sam's family for meals so everyone could get acquainted. They even had her grandfather join them one evening, but there was still the unresolved rift with her grandmother.

Luke left the police station around lunchtime, his thoughts bouncing between the family meeting Alexandra was having this morning and the issue of the missing money from the Blue Santa program. He stepped into the Acorn Café and was hit with the delicious aroma of baked goods and a touch of dread about talking to Gwen. He had accepted her invitation to meet him for lunch only because he'd decided to tell her he didn't see their relationship going beyond friendship. The regular kind of friends with *no* benefits.

Gwen sat in a booth near the back and waved when he looked her way. She was a very pretty woman. Blonde, petite but curvy, and with big beautiful eyes. All things he would have been very interested in only a month ago, but after knowing Alexandra, Gwen Clark held no appeal for him.

He stopped to let an elderly couple get up and

pass by and had a moment of second thoughts. Once Alexandra was back in New York, would his attitude about Gwen change? Would he suddenly get lonely and realize she was someone he wanted to date after all?

No. He didn't think so. He continued to her table. "Good afternoon."

"Hi. Thank you for meeting me, Luke."

He slid into the opposite side of the booth. "Sure. What's up?"

"Well…" She glanced at her hands and pressed her lips together nervously. "When I first came to town, I hoped we might hang out together and… have fun. But I've come to realize, that for a couple of reasons, we would be best as friends, and I'm pretty sure you feel the same."

"I, um… Friends." He was so thrown off by her statement that he stumbled over his words like a bumbling idiot.

Gwen chuckled. "I see the way you look at your Alexandra."

"She's not *mine*." But he wanted her to be.

"You know what I mean. I can only hope to have a man look at me that way one day."

"While I agree that we'll be best as friends, unfortunately, Alexandra lives in New York City. A relationship with her is not possible."

"That's ridiculous." She waved a hand through the air. "Haven't you ever heard of long-distance relationships?"

"Haven't you heard that those never work out?"

"Unless they are meant to be. You said she has family here, so that probably means she'll come back."

"Why are you encouraging me to have a relationship with her?"

Gwen laughed and shrugged. "I'm a sucker for a good romance."

"Well, I'm happy to have you as a friend. Especially if you're going to be Cody's new doctor. I don't know about you, but I'm starving. Let's eat." Luke waved at the waiter and they ordered lunch.

Alex ran over to the diner to give Sam and Dawn a design she'd been working on for advertisements they wanted to run. After waving to her uncle Sam through the kitchen window, she went into the back office and found Dawn busily typing on the computer.

"Good afternoon. I have those drawings we talked about."

Her aunt took off a pair of reading glasses and sat back in her chair. "Wonderful. Have a seat. I could use a break."

"I can't stay too long." She sat in the chair across from her aunt. "I have to meet Tess at the park to get Cody."

"How are you feeling after that rather emotional family discussion with your grandparents this morning?"

Alex rolled her eyes. "I'm sad people are hurting, and that her actions stole so many years from so many of us, but I also feel sorry for her. I really don't think she had any idea of the consequences of what she was doing."

"I agree." Dawn raised her arms to stretch. "I have to say, your existence came as a shock to all of us. I've known Audrey for years and she's always been a good mother-in-law. I mean, don't get me wrong, she loves to have her hand in everyone's business."

"I got that impression rather quickly, but it seems to come from a place of love."

"It does, but I had no idea your grandmother could lie about something as big as hiding her son's miraculous return from the dead. I don't believe for a second that she would've done such a thing if she had any idea there was a child involved. Family means everything to her."

"It's going to take both of my parents a while before they can forgive her."

"And I don't blame them. She stole a lot from them, but it's nice to see them making up for lost time. They're so loving and sweet together."

"Don't make me think too hard on that subject." Alex covered her ears, making her aunt Dawn laugh.

When Alex came out of the office and went to the counter to get a Coke to go, she saw the back of Luke's head as he sat at a booth in a far corner of the restaurant. Even from behind she knew it was him and was so glad to see him. The morning's family discussion had put a downward emotional spin on her day, and she'd been wanting to tell him about it. She walked his way, intending to slip up behind him and do the guess-who thing, but she'd only gotten halfway when he shifted in his seat, and she saw that there was a woman sitting across from him. A very pretty woman. Gwen Clark. The same one who had hugged him so tightly on several occasions.

A wave of nausea hit her hard and fast. That horrible flash of jealousy that made you want to do things out of your character. Like cause a scene. She froze in place before turning and rushing out of the café.

I'm being ridiculous. I'm leaving Oak Hollow. She's staying. And Luke will move on with his life. Without me.

Alex stopped a few stores down the sidewalk and leaned against the redbrick wall outside Mackintosh's Five and Dime. Cody needed a mother and Luke needed a good woman in his life. And Gwen seemed like a good option. Smart, accomplished, beautiful, kind.

But the woman had zero sense of fashion.

She shook her head, immediately ashamed of her unkind thought and recognized her jealousy. It was an ugly thing and had no place in this situation, but it cramped her gut and tears stung the backs of her eyes. They had agreed to this friends-with-benefits arrangement while she was here, which would only be for a few more days. But she wished he had at least waited until she was gone before meeting up with another woman. She attempted to stuff down her envy without success and hurried down the sidewalk to where Cody was playing in the park with Hannah. It was going to take her a whole lot longer to move on than she'd anticipated once she returned home.

Home.

Why did Oak Hollow suddenly feel like home? If she was completely honest with herself, she didn't want to leave this quaint little town in the Texas Hill Country. Could she stay?

I need a sign.

Pausing once again, she glanced around the town square as if the answer would leap out and make itself known. Just then her cell phone rang and startled her so much she jumped.

"Hello."

"Good afternoon, Ms. Roth. This is Dr. Carrington. I'm calling to offer you the music-therapist position."

"Wow. That's amazing." The words came out of her mouth, but exhilaration did not rise in her blood as she would've expected only a few weeks ago.

"When do you return from Texas?"

"On August the second."

"Excellent. Can you come in the day after you get home and we can discuss the details?"

"Yes. Absolutely."

They ended the conversation, and she dropped her phone into her purse. She'd asked for a sign, and she couldn't have gotten a more in-the-face one than an offer for the job she'd thought was unattainable. But was it a job she still wanted as much as her heart wanted her to stay in Oak Hollow? With Luke. With Cody.

Before she pushed away from her spot against the wall, Luke and Gwen came out of the Acorn Café, laughing together. Thankfully, they headed in the opposite direction. Speaking to them right now was at the bottom of her list, because hiding her jealousy and aching heart were beyond her acting ability.

Alex and Cody started cooking dinner before Luke got home, and at first, she faked happiness for the little boy's sake, but shortly into their dinner prep, he had her almost back to her usual happy self. Their last few days together needed to be as wonderful as possible, and she planned to give it her all to make that happen.

"How many miles to New York?" The child's questions about her leaving were increasing each day.

"I'm not sure, but no matter how many miles, we can video-chat over the phone or computer." She poured sauce over the meat and handed the empty jar to Cody. "How does that sound?"

"And have sing-alongs?"

"Absolutely."

Cody climbed onto his step stool, rinsed the jar and put it into the recycle bin. He had become her reason for cleaning as she cooked. The kitchen was not in perfect order but no longer needed caution tape, and instead, featured a tub of soapy water in the sink for washing along the way and her personal helper, who retrieved and put items away.

Luke came into the kitchen, gave Cody a high five, and when she didn't turn from the sink to greet him, he kissed her cheek. "Smells good in here."

Knowing her emotional state would show on her face, she couldn't make herself meet his eyes. "How was your day? Anything exciting happen?"

"Just an ordinary day."

She bit her tongue, refusing to ask if lunch with a beautiful woman was *ordinary*. "Dinner is almost ready, but you have time to change out of your uniform."

When he continued to lean against the counter, she crossed to the refrigerator and pretended to look for something. Their conversation sounded like a married couple, and that's the way they'd been living, but it wasn't the truth. This was a part-time, fantasy arrangement, and it was time to face reality.

When she pulled her head out of hiding, Luke was gone, but he returned within minutes, looking comfortable in a pair of faded jeans and a black T-shirt that matched his moody, dark eyes. The boys filled their bowls and took their usual seats at the kitchen table, but as she turned with her food, she slipped and dumped pasta down the front of her body from breasts to toes.

Their laughter was the last straw. An uncomfortable heat rushed up to scald her cheeks and her insides quivered. Alex rushed from the kitchen, down the hallway and closed herself in the bathroom. Let those two hooting monkeys clean up the mess she'd left splattered across the floor. She was emotional, confused about her future and extremely irritable. And, now, covered with tomato sauce.

She peeled off her dirty shirt and dropped it into the bathtub, eager to get out of her clothes and wash the day down the drain. After struggling with the button on her shorts, she yanked off her too tight panties and kicked them across the bathroom.

"Die a slow death, you binding beast."

Her own reaction to the culmination of the day's events suddenly struck her as ridiculously funny. Was she actually threatening to send her panties to hell? She doubled over with belly-deep laughter, tears streaming from her eyes, gasping for air between cackles of hysterical laughter. She'd been the one who'd overindulged on pie and Coca-Cola since arriving in Oak Hollow and couldn't believe she was blaming it on her offending undergarments. She'd buy bigger panties and be happier for it.

The difficult family meeting, seeing Luke with Gwen and accepting a job that no longer held its expected appeal were a lot in one day. She hadn't even told her mom about Dr. Carrington's call, which said a lot. But what truly weighed on her mind was knowing she'd all too soon have to say goodbye to the man and child she loved.

Her head snapped up, and the remains of her laughter faded as she stared at her reflection, blinking helplessly at the image of a woman who'd tumbled headlong.

I'm in love with Luke Walker.

And in addition to the romantic passion for a man, sweet maternal love for a wonderful child had awakened a new area of her heart.

A knock at the bathroom door made her jump.

"Um…are you okay in there, sweetheart?"

Even with his deep voice muffled by the door, she could hear his concern, and possibly a touch of wariness. "Yes. I'm fine. Just need a minute."

Her cleansing burst of emotions combined with standing under a steaming hot shower calmed her enough to think. The father she wanted to know would be in Manhattan with her mother. With her apartment and friends. Where a really good job waited. Returning home was really her only option. Anything else was a fantasy, especially since she'd witnessed Luke already taking steps to move on with his life. And imagine what Luke would think if she admitted to questioning her career path. He might go back to calling her irresponsible and reckless. Alex propped her forehead against the shower's blue tiles and wiped water from her eyes. She shouldn't care what he thought, but she did.

When she opened the bathroom door, Luke was coming out of the bedroom.

"I made you a sandwich. I didn't want you to go to bed hungry, or mad."

His thoughtfulness touched her heart, and she wanted nothing more than to fall into his arms and tell him everything. "I'm not mad. It's just been a..." She ran her hands through her wet hair.

"A hell of a day?" he asked.

"That's one way to put it."

"Come eat. I told Cody he could watch a few more songs on the sing-along tape before his bath."

She followed him into the kitchen and took a seat at the table, where a sandwich and chips waited.

"Want to talk about it?" Luke moved in behind her, working his magic on the muscles of her shoulders.

With her head tilted back against his stomach, she let more tension melt away under his talented fingers. "Is Cody upset that I stormed out before we ate?"

"He's okay. He helped me clean up and said maybe you needed to sort something to calm down."

That made her chuckle. "He's such a sweet boy. I'm really going to miss him."

"We'll both miss you, sweetheart."

The kiss he planted on the top of her head was filled with tenderness, and Alex suddenly needed to be in his arms. She stood, pushed aside her chair and clung to his waist with her head tucked under his chin, soaking in his touch while she still could.

"You know I'll miss you, too. I came to Oak Hollow unsure of what to expect. Then I started making new friends, finding family and learning things about the place my parents met and fell in love. I started having these big dreams of things working out like a Hallmark movie." She left out the part about falling in love with him. "Then... there's this plot twist, and I have a back-from-the-dead father, which is amazing and wonderful. And I have a grandmother who's caused all this pain and heartache. *Not* so wonderful."

He cradled her cheek and tipped her face to meet his gaze. "I'm sorry I didn't ask earlier about your family meeting with your grandparents. That should've been the first thing I did."

"It's okay. I get the feeling there's a lot on your mind and that more went on at work than just the ordinary?"

His sigh was deep, and he began to sway them from side to side, dancing to the beat of their hearts. "Being a small police department, it's difficult when someone you trust does something wrong. You know that missing money problem I mentioned? I think we know who it is, but we need more proof." He tucked a damp curl behind her ear. "But never mind about that right now. I want to hear about your day."

"The family meeting went about like I expected. Everything was laid out, and I guess it was progress, but we're not one big happy family yet. And I'm not sure how that will happen while we're in Manhattan." She pasted on a big fake smile and met his eyes. "In Manhattan, where I'll be working as a music therapist at the Carrington Clinic."

"You got the job?"

"Yes." She searched his face for signs that he was crushed and would beg her to stay, but his expression was blank, giving away nothing. "I got the call...right after lunch."

Right after I saw you moving on with your life.

An unwelcome truth hit Luke with the force of a freight train. He pulled Alexandra into a tight hug, hiding his face in her hair. "That's really great, sweetheart."

She didn't need to see a forced smile, or how her announcement was crushing him. Stupidly, he'd been holding out a secret hope that she'd stay in Oak Hollow. He'd let a daydream get into his head, and now, he'd have to deal with the fallout of his mistake. His own selfishness and lack of self-control were also going to hurt his nephew.

"Dr. Carrington wants me to go see him the day after I get home."

The sweet sound of her voice brought him back to the moment, and he eased out of their embrace. "You're going to be brilliant. I'm so proud of you." His cell phone rang, and like a coward, he used it as an excuse. "Sorry. I need to take this." He left her alone in the kitchen and stepped outside to answer the call from a number he didn't even recognize.

Luke had to start preparing himself for life after the whirlwind that was Alexandra Roth.

Chapter Eighteen

The next morning, Alex and Cody went out to her dad's place in the little blue sports car she'd been driving around the small town. She wanted to tell them about her job offer in hopes that her mom's excitement would spur her own. When she parked, her young sidekick jumped out and ran ahead, eager to play the old acoustic guitar her dad let him use whenever he came over.

Cody waved when her mother welcomed him from her seat on the front porch swing, and then he was through the handcrafted door before Alex had reached the wraparound porch.

"Hi, honey." Kate set her romance novel on a small table fashioned out of a cypress stump and left her spot on the swing. "I'm glad you're here.

Your dad and I were planning to come see you in town today."

"Dr. Carrington called yesterday. I got the job," she blurted out, and was immediately engulfed in a tight hug.

"Congratulations! I'm so proud of you."

"What are we proud about today?" her dad asked from the open doorway.

"Our talented daughter got the job at the Carrington Clinic."

"I'm not a bit surprised." Charlie high-fived Alex. "You take after your beautiful mother in brains and charm."

Kate put an arm around his waist and kissed his cheek, but when she turned back to her daughter, her expression fell. "Alexandra, why aren't you beaming from ear to ear?"

Alex pressed her knuckles hard against her lips and dropped onto one of the rocking chairs. Her chest ached with the combination of surprise at being offered the job and distress that so shortly after discovering love…she'd lose it. The beginner's rhythm of Cody's guitar playing drifted out from inside the cabin, and she was glad he couldn't hear their conversation. "This last month in Oak Hollow has been…eye-opening."

"Talk to us," Kate said and tugged Charlie over to sit on the swing.

Watching her parents made her ache for a *real* relationship with Luke. "I thought I had everything figured out, but I've started to question my future.

I've been all over the place with my career aspirations. Modeling, nanny, art, culinary school, music degree. Why can't I settle down to one thing?"

"I'm always saying you take after your mother, but this is something you get from me. I've tried out lots of different jobs, and my parents didn't like any of them." Charlie motioned to his hand-built home. "Like construction and woodworking. But I want you to do whatever will make you happy."

"We both do," her mother said. "I know how excited you were about getting the music-therapy position. Before coming here, you would've called and told me the moment you got the news. I think you're questioning the location of the job, not the job itself. You need to think, really think about what you want most. What kind of life you want to live. It's okay to change your mind. It's okay to say no to the job at the Carrington Clinic."

Alex's head snapped up to meet her mother's gaze. "You think I should turn down Dr. Carrington's offer?"

"If that's what you want."

"I will admit that when he called and offered the position, I wasn't nearly as excited as I thought I'd be."

"You mean as excited as you would've been before meeting Luke and Cody?" Kate asked.

Her mother had said what she'd been reluctant to voice aloud. "So you're saying I have options, and neither of you will judge me if I turn down this amazing job?"

"Exactly. And this leads nicely into what your dad and I want to talk to you about. An opportunity has presented itself right here in Oak Hollow, and I'm toying with the idea of selling my share of the medical practice and moving here to take over for one of the town doctors."

Alex was momentarily stunned, but once she took a second to let it set in, she realized she wasn't surprised. She'd watched the two of them together, and as a couple they seemed perfectly suited for this small town. "Wow. If that's what you want, I'm all for it. Does that mean selling the apartment?"

"You can have the apartment if you want to stay in Manhattan."

Alex looked out at the thicket of trees swaying in the breeze. Her mother was hinting that she could stay in this beautiful place. The idea sent an instant thrill straight to her heart. There were those job openings for a music and art teacher at the local school district. Could she do it? Should she forgo the job offer in Manhattan? If they sold the apartment, her half would be a good amount to add to her savings and start a new life here with her parents. And if things went as she hoped, it could be the beginning of a life with Luke and Cody.

"Alex, honey, are you okay? You're unusually quiet and staring into space."

"Sorry. I'm fine. Just thinking."

Charlie leaned forward with his elbows braced on his knees. "I'd really love the chance to spend time with you. If you want to take the job, I'll move to Manhattan tomorrow."

"That's right," her mother said. "Relocating here is just one option."

Her heart lightened. She had *two* parents who were both willing to alter their lives for her. "I'm twenty-five years old. You're both acting like I'm a child."

"You *are* my child, and I've missed those twenty-five years. All because…" He waved his hand through the air like he could erase the past. "Never mind about that right now. I just don't want to miss any more time getting to know you. Your mom has been filling me in and is probably getting tired of my questions, but I have so much to catch up on."

"Tell us what you're thinking," Kate requested.

Her parents wanted to start their long-overdue life together, and she knew they really wanted to live in the home her dad had built in the woods outside town, and she couldn't blame them. "I love it here. And I know you do," she said to her dad. "I like seeing how happy the two of you are together, and I don't know how things would be back in Manhattan. I can picture the three of us here in Oak Hollow. I can picture my life here."

Saying it aloud scared the hell out of her. What if Luke wasn't as happy about the prospect of her staying as she was?

Her mother's smile grew, lifting her high cheekbones. "Dr. Clark wants to retire. He has a nurse practitioner already working with him, and she will need a doctor to partner with."

"His niece. Gwen Clark." Alex took a breath to push aside the jealousy and kept quiet about seeing them at the café. "I've met her."

"I don't know if love and loss are fated," her father said and looked between the two women. "But I think life is about timing, and you should go for what you want. Don't let precious time slip away. Grab on to the people and opportunities you want with both hands."

Her father was a wise man, and she intended to take his advice to heart.

Back at Luke's house that evening, Alex swirled one last stroke of blue paint across the sky, then with the tip of the brush caught between her teeth, she sat back in the kitchen table chair to assess her work and liked what she saw. The nature scene evoked the feelings she got when admiring the Texas Hill Country. And adding the silhouette of a couple with a child between them—all of them holding hands as they walked into the sunset—was the perfect touch. Her time in Texas had roused a new version of her artistic muse, one with a broader outlook on the world. Spending time in this place, with these people, and finding her father was more than she'd hoped to get out of this trip. It was life-changing to say the least.

She'd almost said something about possibly staying in Oak Hollow several times since Luke had arrived home from work, but hadn't wanted to bring up the topic in front of Cody. And then he'd been pulled away by Anson's phone call right after the little boy's bedtime.

After washing her brushes, she gathered her supplies, and since her messiness bothered her housemates, she took everything to the bedroom in an attempt to form a habit of putting things away. When she tiptoed back down the hallway past Cody's closed door, she could hear Luke in the living room still talking on the phone. From his side of the conversation, she could tell the two men were in deep discussion about how to handle the problem in their department. She peeked around the corner just as he cursed, crumpled a piece of paper and hurled it across the room, much like she often did.

This was not the best time for a serious conversation about their future. Although excitement tested her patience, she'd wait until the right time to discuss possibly declining the job in Manhattan and staying in Oak Hollow to take a job at the local school district, or maybe even open her own music-therapy practice.

Instead of interrupting, Alex left him to his work and slipped out the kitchen door into the backyard to gaze at the moon. The night was alive with the sounds of crickets and frogs, and a warm wind blew loose strands of hair against her cheeks. In the middle of the backyard, she sunk down onto the grass and…

Her heart flipped and then plummeted. Cody

was on the roof! The breath froze like painful shards of ice in her lungs.

His little legs were hanging off the edge, rhythmically swinging like he didn't have a care in the world. She sprang to her feet and rushed to the ladder Luke had left leaning against the house after cleaning the gutters. Without a second thought about her fear of heights, she climbed to the top. He scooted back from the edge to make room and patted the shingles, inviting her to sit beside him.

"Cody, it's not safe up here. We need to go down." She glanced over her shoulder at the ground below, and the panic struck like a sharp blade. The ladder suddenly felt as if it would dissolve under her, and the whole world wavered unstably. She threw herself forward, pressing her upper body against the roof, and slithered forward on her belly until her whole body was sprawled against the rough shingles, her arms and legs spread wide.

"You're silly," he giggled and pointed to the sky. "Look up."

Cody obviously thought she was pretending, but she was definitely not. Fear radiated from every pore of her being. Ever so slowly, Alex rolled onto her back and clung to a nearby vent pipe. Her heart knocked in her chest and sweat broke out across every inch of her skin, but she had to get herself under control. Getting him safely off the roof was the priority. One breath in, slow and steady. Big breath out, willing the panic away.

"Big, big, big moon." Cody reached skyward

with both hands as if he could pluck it from the heavens.

It was as big and bright as the weatherman had promised and staring at it helped her get herself under a semblance of control. She glanced at the little boy beside her with his thin arms wrapped around his knees and a huge smile on his face.

"Is my mommy in the stars?"

Tears sprang to her eyes and tightened her throat. "I think she is. I bet she's looking down at you right now and is so proud of you."

"Are you from the stars?"

His question surprised her. "I don't think so. I'm too afraid of heights to be from way up there."

He patted her arm. "Don't be scared. I'm with you."

His sweetness and appreciation for the beauty in the world never ceased to inspire and amaze her. And she knew in that moment, there was no question about what direction she wanted to take her life. Alex wanted to stay in Oak Hollow. To continue building a relationship with her father and his family. To watch Cody grow into the wonderful adult she knew he'd be. And to stay and build a life with the man she'd fallen head over heels in love with.

More than any job she could imagine, she wanted to be a part of Luke's and Cody's lives. Forever. Her heart rate sped with joy instead of fear.

Chapter Nineteen

Luke ended his call with Anson and stood to stretch his back and work the tension from his neck. They'd made progress on a plan, but he was still frustrated and irritable. Not just because of the issue at work, but mainly because Alexandra would be leaving soon. She'd take the prestigious job in Manhattan and start her career and a life...without him. He'd known this arrangement between them was temporary the whole time, but still allowed himself to...

No.

He could not allow himself to use the *L* word. But regardless of what word was applied to his feelings, the fact remained that he'd done exactly what he'd promised himself he wouldn't and gotten too close. And, worst of all, he'd allowed Cody to do the same.

Now, they'd both have to readjust to it being only the two of them.

He wanted to find Alexandra, take her to bed and never let her go, and at the same time, find a way to put some distance between them so it wouldn't be so hard when she left. He walked down the hallway to Cody's room for one last nightly check, but when he opened his nephew's door and peeked inside, the bed was empty. He checked the bathroom, the kitchen and his room, but neither of them was in the house. Then he remembered her saying she was planning to go out and see the moon. He looked on the front porch then went out into the backyard. Still not seeing them, he turned in a circle.

"Cody? Alexandra? Are y'all out here?"

"Up here," she called out.

Her voice came from somewhere above, and he spun back in the direction of the house. They were on the roof! His shock and fury were instant and strong. He scrambled up the ladder and found Alex sprawled out like a starfish and Cody smiling at the sky.

"What the hell were you thinking bringing Cody up onto the roof?" He hissed the words through gritted teeth and then continued without giving her a chance to respond. "How could you be so irresponsible and think this was okay?" When she didn't seem inclined to answer, he glanced at his nephew's astonished little face. Cody had been smiling in a way Luke rarely saw, but he'd ended that with his harsh words to Alexandra.

Great. Just great. She swoops in here and wins Cody's affections. She shows him some magical good time, and I get to come in and be the adult that ends his fun.

But being on the roof was not safe for a little boy. "Scoot on your bottom to me, buddy. It's time to get off the roof."

"No." Cody shook his head of dark hair and motioned to the sky. "Look up, Uncle Luke. A big, big, big moon."

"We can look at the moon from the ground. Please, come to me. I really need you to do what I'm asking." Thank the heavens he moved toward him and didn't throw a fit in such a dangerous spot. Luke shot a steely glance at the woman who was lying leisurely and staring up at the sky. The one who wouldn't meet his eyes or even raise her head. "We'll talk after I get him inside."

One rung at a time, he stepped down with his nephew tucked between his body and the wooden ladder. Safely back on the ground, he kneeled before him. "Look at the moon one more time then we need to go inside, change into clean PJs and get you back into bed." He hoped giving Cody a list of the steps would make the transition easier and hold off a meltdown. But when his nephew stared up at him, crossed his thin arms and dug in his heels, Luke knew it hadn't worked this time. "What's wrong?"

"You have to save Alexandra."

"She doesn't need saving." He was the one that

needed saving from the heartache and loneliness that would settle in once she left.

"I'm okay, Cody," she called down from above. "Don't worry about me. Go inside with your uncle Luke and you can dream about the moon."

Luke paused and glanced up. She didn't really sound okay—her voice was shaky and hoarse. He almost asked her what was wrong, but instead, he decided he'd finish this conversation when young ears couldn't hear what he had to say about her putting his nephew in danger.

After glancing between his uncle and up toward the woman on the roof, Cody followed Luke inside. As he worked to put on clean pajamas, the young boy continued to look around as if something scary would jump out at any moment. "I went up the ladder," he repeated three times and almost fell trying to get his leg into his pajama pants.

"I know you did, but that was a dangerous thing to do." He helped him get his foot through the bottom of the tight pants leg and sat on the bed as Cody climbed under the covers. He couldn't shake the feeling that he held some of the responsibility because he'd left the ladder out. "Remember when we talked about not leaving the house if it's dark outside?"

Cody nodded, but wouldn't look at him.

"I was scared when I couldn't find you."

"Uncle Luke, go get Alexandra. Promise?"

"I will. I promise. I love you, buddy. Good night." He kissed the little boy's forehead and stood.

"Don't forget Alexandra."

"I won't." Luke would never forget her, and that was a big part of his problem and foul mood.

When he left the bedroom, she still hadn't come inside, no doubt because she knew he was furious. He marched outside in full officer mode and stood at the foot of the ladder. "We need to talk."

"Okay." Her voice trembled.

He waited, cross and impatient, but there was no sign that she was even making a move to climb down the ladder. "Are you coming down?"

"Can't do that right now."

"What do you mean *can't*? I don't want to yell up at you."

"Then. Stop. Yelling."

He scrubbed a hand across his mouth, growing more exasperated by the second. When she still didn't move, he climbed up enough to brace his arms on the edge of the roof and found her in the exact same position. "I don't know what's going on with you, but you're acting like a spoiled child. I knew you were irresponsible and reckless but taking him up on this roof is unacceptable. Don't you realize the danger you put him in?" All of his frustration had gathered and was pouring out in a fountain of admonishment. He waited for a response, any response, but she remained silent and motionless. "You're just lying there, moon gazing with stars in your eyes. Real life isn't a *Mary Poppins* movie. It's not a silly musical where everything turns out fine and dandy. Real life is hard and brutal and kicks you when you're down."

Just like knowing and missing you is going to tear me up for who knows how long!

She put a hand to her chest and mumbled incoherently, but still didn't make a move to get off the roof.

"Fine. I'll take him to stay with Tess tomorrow morning." He jumped off the middle of the ladder, stormed into the house and grabbed a beer from the refrigerator. Just to make sure, he double-checked that Cody was still in his bed and then went into the bathroom and locked the door. He wanted a long hot shower to ease his tension, but instead, he leaned against the counter and sipped his beer.

He'd broken his promise to his nephew and left her on the roof, but what was he supposed to do? He couldn't force her to behave in a responsible manner—or stay in Texas—just because he wished it.

Alex continued to lay motionless on the roof, not because she was terrified of the height, but because she felt empty. And crushed. And hollow. As if her heart was bleeding, her happiness and future plans of only moments ago seeping out onto the shingles beneath her. How—after their days and nights together—could he say such things? How could he possibly believe she'd knowingly risk Cody's safety?

His hurtful words replayed on a painful loop. Spoiled. Reckless. Irresponsible. That life kicks you when you're down. Well, he'd sure managed to kick the wind out of her. She'd been so busy trying to overcome her fear of heights, and so shocked at his statements, that she hadn't even spoken up to defend herself.

But if he could believe these things about her, he wasn't the man she'd thought. Luke had told Cody that she didn't need saving. And she didn't, but she wanted a man who *wanted* to. A man who thought highly of her and trusted that she'd do the right thing.

A broken bone couldn't hurt as badly as she already did, and she no longer cared if she fell off the roof. Alex sat up, scooted carefully to the edge and, after a deep breath, made her way slowly and steadily down to the ground. Nausea hit her, and she leaned against the side of the house. Once the roiling subsided, she carried the ladder to the garage and put it safely away.

Not wanting to run in to Luke, she peered through the kitchen window, and when she saw the room was empty, slipped quietly inside the back door, the words *reckless* and *irresponsible* echoing in her brain. Seeing disappointment on his face would crush her right now. Plus, she was angry enough to say something she couldn't take back— much like he'd done to her. The bathroom door was closed, and she jumped when a cabinet door banged from within. A second later, the water started running. Since he usually took long showers, she had a few minutes to decide what to do.

She went into Cody's room, sat on his bed and found him still awake. "You should be sleeping, sugar boy."

"Are you still scared?"

"No. I'm all better. You don't have to worry about me." She brushed his hair from his forehead. "Tomorrow morning you get to go play with Hannah."

"Why?"

"So you can have fun. She misses you. Cody, I need to go see my mom tonight, but your uncle is here. He's in the shower right now."

He rolled over and faced the wall. "It's Uncle Luke's fault you're leaving. He yelled at you."

No longer able to hold back tears, they trickled down her cheeks. "Don't be mad at your uncle. He loves you very, very much, and he only wants to protect you and make sure you're okay. It scared him that you were on the roof. That's why he yelled."

"No yelling. That's what Uncle Luke says."

"I know, and I'm sure he's sorry." She had no doubt he was sorry about upsetting Cody, but as far as she was concerned…she was no longer sure.

"Are you leaving Oak Hollow?"

"Not yet. Tonight, I'm only going to Charlie's house to see my mom, but remember we marked the day on the calendar when I have to fly back to New York?"

"The day that has the sad face on it?"

"Yes, but I'll see you before I fly home." She bit her lip, hoping she hadn't just lied to him. Surely Luke wouldn't keep her from seeing Cody before she left. "Even when I do go home, we can talk on the phone anytime you want. Can I give you a hug?"

The little boy sat up, keeping his arms against his sides, but leaned his body and head against her.

She gently hugged him and kissed the top of his head. "I love you, sugar boy. I'll see you very soon. Get some sleep and have sweet dreams."

"Okay." He lay down and yawned. "Will you come back if Uncle Luke is nice again?" Another jaw-cracking yawn.

"I'll come back to see you, and we'll play some music."

"Music, music." His eyes drifted closed. "Music."

Alex kissed his forehead, hurried into Luke's bedroom and stuffed the barest essentials into a bag. The shower turned off just as she rushed down the hallway and slipped out the front door. She ran down the sidewalk but stopped a block down Cherry Tree Lane to pull out her phone and call her mother.

"Hello, honey."

"Mom..." That's the only word she got out before she burst into tears.

"What's wrong?"

"He's an ass. A big, dumb ass. Can you come get me?"

"Of course. Where are you?"

She continued walking and gave her location.

"Don't hang up," her mom said. "Tell me what Luke did to have you this upset."

"I don't know where to start."

"Just start at the beginning. Was he not happy to hear that you might stay in Oak Hollow?"

"I didn't even have a chance to tell him. He thinks I'm irresponsible and reckless. He doesn't—" She stumbled over a rock, almost dropped her phone and sat down on the sidewalk. "He doesn't want me around Cody."

"What? That doesn't sound right at all," Kate said. "Are you sure you didn't misunderstand something? Or maybe he's the one who misunderstood?"

Alex took a breath and tried to take her mom's words to heart. She knew he'd been frightened for his nephew, much like the time he'd overreacted when he found them running through the sprinkler. But then he'd hardly known her. Now, he'd had plenty of time to see her with Cody and should know she would never put him in harm's way.

Once her dad's Jeep pulled up, she climbed into the back seat. "Thanks for coming to get me."

"Do I need to go kick his butt?" Charlie asked.

"No. I can do it myself if I decide it needs doing."

Her dad barely held back a chuckle. "That's my girl. I think she gets that attitude from me."

Chapter Twenty

Luke came out of the bathroom and glanced down the hallway. The bedroom door had been open before his shower, and now it was closed. So she'd slipped in and hidden herself away to avoid him? Fine. He didn't feel like talking, anyway. But as he sat on the couch staring at a television that wasn't even turned on, he recalled some of the things he'd said to her. Had he overreacted and been too harsh, like the time he'd found them in the sprinkler and jumped to the wrong conclusion?

A sinking feeling engulfed him, and he quickly made his way to his bedroom and knocked. "Can we talk?" Seconds ticked by with no response. "Alexandra, please." Luke tried the knob and, finding it unlocked, he opened the door. The dresser drawer she'd been using was open and half-empty, a trail of clothing leading to the bed…but she was not in the room.

"What the hell? Where is she?"

He once again rushed through the house like he'd done while searching for Cody. Outside, he noticed she'd put away the ladder, but it was as if the woman herself had vanished. A heaviness squeezed his heart, and he tugged at the collar of his shirt. Was this how it was going to feel when she went home?

I'm not ready.

Would he ever be ready for her to leave? His brain quickly answered. No, he wouldn't. When his phone call went to voice mail, he sent a text.

Where are you?

He stared at the phone, waiting for those three little dots to pop up and assure him she was responding. Finally, the dots bounced rhythmically on the screen but disappeared with no message.

I'm worried. Please let me know you're okay.

Still nothing, except the actual sound of crickets in the trees and the pounding of his own heart. "I've really screwed up this time."

As much as he wanted to, he didn't dare wake Cody to ask questions about the roof incident. Instead, he returned to his seat on the couch and called Charlie.

"What'd you do, Walker?" Charlie said in place of hello.

"I screwed up. Is Alexandra with you?"

"Yep. I've got her."

"She won't answer my calls or texts. Is she okay?"

"Yes, but she's sure mad at you. She's in another room talking to her mom, and I only know bits and pieces of what happened."

"I found her and Cody on the roof and got upset that she'd put him in danger."

"Wait. Alexandra was on the roof?" Charlie's voice was filled with shock. "I've talked to her about our shared fear of heights, and hers is worse than mine. I have a hard time believing she wanted to go up on the roof."

"I didn't know she was afraid of heights. Then why would she…?" All the pieces started to form a picture. Cody saying to save her. Her not moving or speaking. "Well, crap. Can I talk to her?"

"She and Kate have the door closed, and I don't feel comfortable interrupting. When they come out, I'll tell her you want to talk, but you might need to give her a little time."

Luke sighed deeply, frustrated but thankful she was safe. "Okay."

"I'll look after her. Don't you worry."

After they hung up, he continued to glance at his phone every few minutes. They only had a few days left before she returned to New York, and he'd gone and pulled this bonehead move. His brief thought about putting distance between them had materialized almost instantaneously in an epically bad way. For hours, he alternated between pacing the house, brooding in one spot or another and opening and closing the refrigerator before he fell asleep on the couch.

He woke with Cody looking down at him. "Hey, buddy, you okay?"

"She's gone." Cody crossed his arms and glared at his uncle. "I'm mad at you."

His nephew's words struck like a whip. "I'm mad at me, too." He sat up and rubbed sleep from his eyes. "Did you go onto the roof all by yourself or did Alexandra help you?"

The little boy looked at his bare feet then at the ceiling. "I went up the ladder first. To see the big, big, big moon."

"And she went outside and found you on the roof?"

"Yep. And she got scared. I took care of her."

Luke's stomach roiled.

"I'm mad!" Cody stomped his foot, ran to his bedroom and slammed the door hard enough that a picture rattled on the wall.

"Freaking great." Luke sighed. The only positive in this situation was that his nephew was finally using words to express himself. He grabbed his phone from the coffee table, but there was still no message. Even though it was only six in the morning, he sent another text and then placed a call that went straight to voice mail. Thank goodness it was his day off, which made his threat to send Cody over to Tess's an empty one.

Luke made a pot of coffee and ached for the sight of her dancing around and making a mess as she cooked. He missed her singing. He missed her scent. Hell, he even missed her trail of things spread over every surface. The items that let him know she was there. He took his cup of coffee, went down the hall and opened Cody's door. His nephew sat at his desk with a crayon in hand.

"What are you doing, buddy?"

"A picture for Alexandra. You need to say sorry, Uncle Luke."

"You're right, and I plan to do just that."

In his bedroom, her guitar was still in the corner, and he sighed with relief. She wouldn't leave Oak Hollow without it. But soon, too soon, all her things would be gone, and she'd be almost two thousand miles away. He sat on the bed and caught the scent of her. How long would it be before her sweetness no longer lingered? The ache that settled into his chest wasn't the devastation he'd felt at Libby's death, but it echoed with some of the same pain. He couldn't let her go without making things right. He didn't know exactly what that would entail, but he'd figure it out.

He dressed quickly and stuck his head into Cody's room. "Get some clothes on, please. I'm going to take you over to see Hannah and then I'm going to go and tell Alexandra I'm sorry."

* * *

After only a few hours of sleep, Alex sat bleary-eyed on the front porch of her dad's cabin, hoping her mug of coffee would wake her up enough for some clarity. Unlike the view on Cherry Tree Lane, Charlie's property was secluded with not a house in sight and only thick trees stretching out before her. The surroundings should have been immensely peaceful, but heavy cloud cover and trees dripping from the rainstorm created a dreary scene that fit her even darker mood.

Talking to her mother until the wee hours had helped, and even though he'd used some of the same hurtful words, she knew Luke was nothing like her ex-boyfriend, Thomas, but Alex was having trouble getting into her normally understanding and forgiving mood. Having her plans toppled by Luke's outburst before she could even reveal them was throwing her thoughts into uncertainty. And there was a lot to consider. Career decisions. The question of her future home address. How to make sure her sweet Cody was okay. The unexpected whirlwind romance that was breaking her heart. And her parents' happiness.

Even though they pretended otherwise, there was no doubt their first choice was to live in Oak Hollow. Considering their twenty-five-year heartache, her mom and dad deserved the life they'd been denied, but Alex wasn't sure how to live in this small town and frequently see Luke if they weren't a couple. She drank the last of her coffee and searched for the strength to make the right decisions. The least she could do was suffer a little of her own pain for their sake. She needed to get her mom settled in Texas, no matter where she eventually ended up. Maybe she could live here part-time and in Manhattan the rest. But that thought brought her back to the problem of a job.

A vehicle rumbled in the distance, and a moment later Luke's truck came around the curve of the dirt driveway. She stayed rooted in the chair and fought the urge to go to him as he came up onto the porch. He rubbed a hand over his jaw, the stubble rasping under his fingers. It was just the right amount of scruff to be sexy, and she hated herself for even noticing.

"Can we talk?" he asked.

Knowing how emotions played in his eyes, she refused to meet his gaze lest it weaken her resolve. "You said plenty last night."

"I know. And I'm really sorry about that. Truly."

Sincerity rang in his voice, but she did not respond to his apology. Not this time. She was hurt and still mad enough to make him beg, just a little.

"Alexandra, why did you go up onto the roof?"

"Why do you think, dumbass? To get Cody. When I saw his little legs dangling over the side, my heart dropped." A shudder worked through her body, and she wrapped her arms around her middle. "I was up the ladder before I thought about what I was doing. Then the panic hit."

"Why didn't you tell me you were afraid of

heights when I came up the ladder? Why didn't you tell me to shut up? It's not like you to just lie there and be so quiet." He kneeled on the wooden planks at her feet and tried to take her hand, but she pulled it from his grasp.

If he touched her, she might be tempted to forgive him too quickly, and if there was a chance of them working this out, he had to know she was serious about her expectations. She would not let another guy treat her or talk to her the way her ex-boyfriend had.

"You're right. I'm a dumbass," he said.

"I won't disagree. Do you even remember the things you said to me?"

He winced, shoved his fingers through his hair and sat in the chair beside her. "Some of them."

"Shall I refresh your memory? You insinuated that I live in a musical fantasyland. You accused me of putting Cody in danger. You called me irresponsible. Reckless." Her voice choked up. "That I'm not fit to take care of Cody. If you can think those things about me after all we've shared…" Saying everything aloud refreshed the painful feelings. "I'm not ready to talk to you." She stood and skirted around his legs on her way to the front door.

"Alexandra, please don't go." He jumped to his feet. "I don't believe any of those terrible things. I was scared for Cody and let my stupid mouth get away from me. Let me make this right. What will it take to prove how sorry I am?"

"I don't know. I…" She couldn't find the right

words to tell him how hurt she was that he hadn't believed in her, but she paused on the threshold. "I hope you'll let me see Cody again."

"Of course. Come home with me, and we can work this out. Please."

His pleading expression almost made her give in, but she had to be strong. "I just need you to give me a little more time." She stumbled over the threshold and rushed into the house.

Before Luke could decide what to do next, Charlie came outside and took a seat in one of the rocking chairs.

"Give her time, Walker. She's just protecting herself."

Luke sagged onto the swing and dropped his head into his hands, wishing he could kick his own butt. "I screwed up. I haven't got the sense God gave a turnip."

"That's because you're a man who's given away his heart."

"What?" Luke's head snapped up.

"You heard me. When did you realize you loved my daughter?"

His mouth open and closed and then he sat up ramrod-straight. There was no more denying that he was in love with Alexandra Roth. Was it that obvious to those around him? "I think it was the day I met her, but I fought it."

Charlie made a sound of understanding in his throat and nodded. "Must be something about those

Roth women. I fell in love with Kate just as quickly. Saw her one morning sitting under a tree reading one of those romance novels she loves, and by that night, I was head over heels."

"It was my birthday, and I didn't want to have a party," Luke said. "And even though she'd only been there a few minutes and didn't know a soul, she was ready to send everyone home if that's what I needed." He closed his eyes and pulled up the memory of her standing in the middle of his living room with her hands on her hips, ready to announce the party was over.

"So what do you plan to do about making my daughter happy?"

He focused on the father of the woman he loved. "I plan to do everything in my power to make up for my mistake. To let her know how much I love her. Cody and I want her to be part of our lives. Forever." His true feeling spilled out, and saying it aloud lifted his spirits with hope.

Charlie smiled and nodded. "Good to hear. I think you're going to need one of those grand gestures. Something that will melt her heart. But first, I need a promise from you." His eyes narrowed. "Will you treat her like the most precious thing in the world?"

"Yes, sir. Absolutely."

"Then I'll let you in on a development." He leaned closer and dropped his voice to a whisper. "Kate and Alexandra are thinking about moving to Oak Hollow."

"Really?" The oppressive weight lifted from his chest. "That's the best news I've heard in ages." An idea struck, and he pulled his keys from his pocket. "I know what to do. Can you get her over to my house this evening?"

"I think that's doable."

"I'll call you," he said over his shoulder as he rushed down the steps to his truck.

Chapter Twenty-One

Alex was lying facedown on the bed in her dad's guestroom, regretting walking away while Luke had been trying to apologize. She'd made her point, and it was time to listen, and not act like the spoiled child he'd accused her of being.

Kate sat beside her daughter and stroked her hair like she'd done when she was little. "I'm going to repeat some of what I said last night because I'm not sure what you actually heard. I missed out on so many years with the man I love, and although it wasn't my fault, it does give me some experience to speak from. So tell me, are you in love with Luke?"

She rolled over and scooted up against the head-board. "Yes, and I thought he might love me, too."

"I believe he does. I've watched the two of you.

Do you think he'd be making this much of an effort if he was ready for you to leave?"

Her mother's words echoed her thoughts. He'd called, texted and come out first thing this morning. If he was ready to move on with someone new once she left, why would he go to this trouble? "I think I'm being extra hard on him because I needed to make a point. If there's a chance we can have a serious relationship, I want him to know how I expect to be treated."

"As you should."

A knock sounded, and Charlie stuck his head through the open doorway. "Sorry, but I couldn't help overhearing that last bit, and I totally agree. In fact, that's something Luke and I just talked about." He sat on the foot of the bed. "And don't think I'm trying to take sides with what I say next, because I just want to see things work out between the two of you. I've seen Luke lose his parents, his sister, then take on parenting and do a damn good job of it. He's a good man."

"You're right." Alex swallowed the lump in her throat, feeling guilty about adding to his stress by running away and refusing to listen. "Luke is a great father and has been through a lot more than I can comprehend."

"With the tragedies he's experienced, I would imagine loss is harder for him than most." Kate shifted on the bed and leaned her head against Charlie's shoulder. "Since he still believes you're returning to New York, his behavior could be an unconscious reaction.

"For a long time after losing your mother, I turned my back on love. Having you two in my life has reopened my eyes and heart to things I pushed away. I can see the love when you and Luke look at one another. I see it when you look at the little boy that comes as a package deal."

"Cody is a bonus!" Alex said quickly, her outburst proving to all of them how she truly felt.

"That's a much better way to put it," her dad said and squeezed her foot. "Discovering you are my daughter is the best bonus surprise in the whole world. And having Kate back in my life..." He wrapped an arm around the woman he loved and kissed her cheek. "I can not only see love again, but I can feel it in a way I haven't allowed myself to over the years."

Her parents shared the kind of look that proved true love exists. Is that what they'd seen between her and Luke? It gave her hope for the future.

"There's one more thing," Charlie said. "Before Luke left, he asked me to see if I can talk you into going over to his house this evening."

"Really?" Her pulse fluttered.

"Is that something you want to do?" he asked. "He's supposed to call me later, and if you're not ready, I can—"

"Tell him I'll be there." She scrambled off the bed. "Mom, I need to use your shampoo."

* * *

Luke knew when to ask for help, and luckily, he knew where to start. Fifteen minutes after his call to Tess, she arrived at his house with Anson, Nan and both children. Jenny got there five minutes later. After a brief and embarrassing explanation of what had happened the night before, he prepared to tell them his plan to follow the outlandish fairy-tale design Alexandra had drawn to tease him.

He spread her drawings across the dining room table. "I want to get as much of this as I can done by tonight. I have to win back the woman I love."

"I knew it." Tess squealed and clapped her hands. "Well, then, let's have a look at these."

There was general agreement that they should create Alexandra's design in his backyard. The kids were disappointed the treehouse wouldn't be ready today, the women gushed at the romance of the idea and Anson chuckled and slapped him on the back with an all-too-knowing shake of his head. Luke figured he deserved it after the teasing he'd given Anson when he'd fallen for his wife.

"Time to get started," Tess said. "I have an entire box of white lights in the attic. Jenny, if we make a list, will you go to the garden center?"

"I can do that. I love making lists." With a note-pad and pen she'd pulled from her purse, Jenny took notes as they talked.

"I'll play music," Cody said and circled the adults with Hannah trailing right behind him, clapping and singing "Ring Around the Rosie."

Within minutes, everyone had an assignment and knew what to do. Luke took a moment to observe the friends who were ready to drop everything and help him. He had some awesome people in his life, and if he was able to win back the woman he loved, he'd be one of the luckiest men in town.

By early evening, the yard had been transformed into a rushed version of Alexandra's fairyland vision. He'd called Charlie three times to check that she was still coming, and now, all he could do was hold out hope for the future he envisioned.

The sun had finally set, and Alex fidgeted in the back seat of the Jeep, nervous, anxious and excited. Her dad had insisted she had to wait until the appointed time to go over and talk to Luke. Something was going on, but Charlie wouldn't give her any details. They pulled up in front of Luke's house just as Anson, Tess, Nan and Hannah drove away, all of them waving and wearing big cheesy grins, as if they had a secret.

Alex leaned in and looked between her parents in the front seat. "What's going on?"

"I think it's what's called a grand gesture," her dad said. "You know, one of those things that happen in your romance novels." He chuckled at their shocked expressions. "And you thought I wasn't paying attention when you talk about stories you're reading."

She shared a smile with her mother. "I can see

why you never found anyone that could compare to *my* dad."

"You said that?" he asked Kate.

"Don't let it inflate your head." She softened her jest with a kiss and then turned to her daughter. "Go talk to Luke. I think you have one of the other good ones right inside that house. Listen to your heart."

"I've already forgiven him." A lovely warmth filled her chest, and she didn't even know what he had planned yet. "But I'll gladly take whatever gesture he's offering. You two go do something fun. I'll be fine."

"Call us if you need us," her parents said in unison and then grinned at one another.

They seemed to be thoroughly enjoying team parenting their adult child, and Alex was more than happy to allow them their fun. She climbed out of the Jeep and waved as they drove away. Cody's piano playing could be heard halfway up the front walk. She slipped inside and ached to cuddle him tight against her heart. His little head was tipped to the side as he played with more skill than a five-year-old should possess. But Luke was nowhere in sight.

"Hey, sugar boy. That sounds great."

He sprang off the bench and bounced on his toes. "Come see. Come see."

She followed him through the house to the backyard and gasped at the sight before her. White lights twinkled throughout the trees and across the back fence. Paper butterflies, flowers and Mason jars with tealights hung from branches. Beside the bird feeder she and Cody had bought stood a birdbath with a dancing pixie in the center. The grass had once again been mowed into unusual designs, and a winding path of stepping-stones led to a wrought-iron bench under the tree she'd named Fairy Oak.

Luke stood under its branches, looking extremely handsome in a dark green button-up and a nervous smile. Cody ran ahead and climbed onto the bench, holding up a hand to see if he matched his uncle's height.

She let free her laughter, and the tension eased from Luke's handsome face. "This is so beautiful. You did all this for me?"

"I wanted to make your dream come true. I want to make all of your dreams come true, sweetheart."

In the twilight hour, with hundreds of twinkling lights, it was as if a gossamer thread tethered them. This time she accepted his outstretched hand, loving the heat and strength of his touch, and the spark it sent to her heart. "You do?"

"I really do. And I'm so sorry about the hurtful things I said. Please give me the chance to prove what you mean to me. What you mean to us." He winked at his nephew.

Cody giggled. "Uncle Luke promised to be a good boy."

"Did he?"

"Yes, I did." He squeezed her hand. "I love you, Alexandra Roth."

Hearing those three beautiful words erased the

last traces of doubt. "Officer Luke Walker, I love you, too." The kiss he placed on the back of her hand was old-fashioned romance at its best, sending a whole new batch of flutters dancing through her.

"I want you to follow your heart, and if it leads you to the career in Manhattan, we'll find a way."

Before she could tell him that she'd turned down the job, Cody slipped his fingers into her free hand.

"I don't want you to be my Mary Poppins anymore because she leaves. You be Maria from *The Sound of Music* because she stays. She stays to be the mommy."

So much love swelled inside of her that her vision blurred with an instant sheen of tears. She shot Luke a questioning glance, not wanting to announce her desire to become Cody's mother without first knowing his feelings on the matter. His smile and nod were the confirmation needed.

Alex kissed the child's forehead. "Sugar boy, I love you, and I'm not going anywhere." She brought their hands to her chest. "I turned down the job this morning. I'm moving to Oak Hollow." Her words were barely out before Luke cupped her face and kissed her.

"That's the best news ever. I know it might be too soon, but—"

"Will you be my new mommy?" Cody interrupted and tugged on his uncle's pocket. "Can we give it to her now, Uncle Luke?"

"Hold on, buddy." He chuckled and ruffled the eager child's hair. "I'm getting to it." With a deep breath, he focused on Alexandra. "Please don't think I'm trying to rush you. I just want to make our intentions known. I want you to be part of our lives. Forever." After a shared nod, Cody hopped off the bench, pulled something from Luke's pocket and they dropped to a knee before her. "If you say yes, we can wait as long as you want."

Her heart sped to a rate only true love could bring. "And what is the question?"

"Will you marry me? Will you be my wife?"

"And my mommy?" Cody opened his hand, an emerald-cut diamond ring glinting in his little palm.

She met the intense gazes of the men she loved, her future shining in their eyes. Alexandra put a hand on each of their cheeks. "I would love to be your mommy. And I would love to be your wife."

Luke took the ring from Cody and slipped it onto her trembling finger. "This belonged to my mother and then my sister."

"It's absolutely gorgeous, and it means so much to know who wore it before me," she said through a grin so big that her cheeks ached.

Luke lifted Cody onto his hip and pulled her into a shared embrace. In that moment, they went from something's missing to a family of three.

* * * * *

COMING NEXT MONTH FROM

H HARLEQUIN
SPECIAL EDITION

#2845 A BRAMBLEBERRY SUMMER
The Women of Brambleberry House • by RaeAnne Thayne
Rosa Galvez's attraction to Officer Wyatt Townsend is as powerful as the moon's pull on the tides. But with her past, Rosa knows better than to act on her feelings. Yet her solo life is slowly becoming a sun-filled family adventure—until dark secrets threaten to break like a summer storm.

#2846 THE RANCHER'S SUMMER SECRET
Montana Mavericks: The Real Cowboys of Bronco Heights
by Christine Rimmer
Vanessa Cruise is spending her summer working in Bronco. Rekindling her short-term fling with the hottest rancher in town? Not on her to-do list. But the handsome rancher promises to keep their relationship hidden from the town gossips, then finds himself longing for more. Convincing Vanessa he's worth the risk might be the hardest thing he's ever had to do...

#2847 THE MAJOR GETS IT RIGHT
The Camdens of Montana • by Victoria Pade
Working with Clairy McKinnon on her father's memorial tests Major Quinn Camden's every resolve! Clairy is still hurt that General McKinnon mentored Quinn over his own adoring daughter. When their years-long rivalry is replaced by undeniable attraction, Quinn wonders if the general's dying wish is the magic they both need... or if the man's secrets will tear them apart for good.

#2848 NOT THEIR FIRST RODEO
Twin Kings Ranch • by Christy Jeffries
The last thing Sheriff Marcus King needs is his past sneaking back into his present. Years ago, Violet Cortez-Hill disappeared from his life, leaving him with unanswered questions—and a lot of hurt. Now the widowed father of twins finds himself forced to interact with the pretty public defender daily. Is there still a chance to saddle up and ride off into their future?

#2849 THE NIGHT THAT CHANGED EVERYTHING
The Culhanes of Cedar River • by Helen Lacey
Winona Sheehan and Grant Culhane have been BFFs since childhood. So when Winona's sort-of-boyfriend ditches their ill-advised Vegas wedding, Grant is there. Suddenly, Winona trades one groom for another—and Grant's baby is on the way. With a years-long secret crush fulfilled, Winona wonders if her husband is ready for a family...or firmly in the friend zone.

#2850 THE SERGEANT'S MATCHMAKING DOG
Small-Town Sweethearts • by Carrie Nichols
Former Marine Gabe Bishop is focused on readjusting to civilian life. So the last thing he needs is the adorable kid next door bonding with his dog, Radar. The boy's guardian, Addie Miller, is afraid of dogs, so why does she keep coming around? Soon, Gabe finds himself becoming her shoulder to lean on. Could his new neighbors be everything Gabe never knew he needed?

YOU CAN FIND MORE INFORMATION ON UPCOMING HARLEQUIN TITLES,
FREE EXCERPTS AND MORE AT HARLEQUIN.COM.

HSECNM0621

"Everyone has secrets, do they not? Some they share with
those they trust, some they prefer to keep to themselves."

He was quiet for a long moment. "I hope you know
that if you ever want to share yours, you can trust me."

She trusted very few people. And she certainly wasn't
going to trust Wyatt, who was only a temporary tenant
and would be out of her life in a few short weeks.

"If I had any secrets, I might do that. But I don't. I'm
a completely open book."

She tried for a breezy smile but could tell he wasn't
at all convinced. In fact, he looked slightly disappointed.

She tried to ignore her guilt and opted to change the subject instead. "The lightning seems to have stopped for now. I am sure the power will be back on soon."

"No doubt."

"Thank you again for coming to my rescue. Good night. Be careful going back down the stairs."

"I will do that. Good night."

He studied her, his features unreadable in the dim light of her flashlight. He looked as if he wanted to say something else. Instead, he shook his head slightly.

"Good night."

As he turned to go back down the stairs, the masculine scent of him swirled to her. She felt that sudden wild urge to kiss him again but ignored it. Instead, she went into her darkened apartment, her dog at her heels, and firmly closed the door behind her. If only she could close the door to her thoughts as easily.

Don't miss
A Brambleberry Summer *by RaeAnne Thayne,*
available July 2021 wherever
Harlequin Special Edition books and ebooks are sold.

Harlequin.com